WHISKEY AND PICKLES

A Collection of Short Fiction

Tony Chalk

ISBN: 1533664684
ISBN 13: 9781533664686

DEDICATION

This work is dedicated to someone who has stood steadfastly by my side in the good times, the bad times, and the really bad times. She is my inspiration, my love, and my very sweetest, dearest, and best friend. To my darling wife, Leila.

FOREWORD
DIFFERENT BREEDS

Of course the inevitable question has been, why the name Whiskey and Pickles? It so happened, one evening while I was writing one of the stories contained in this volume, I was drinking my favorite brand of Irish Whiskey and was overcome by a craving for my favorite pickles. Not one to deny myself the simple pleasures in life, I indulged. The thought of the strange combination stuck in my head and as I was putting the puzzle together that was to be this book, it occurred to me that putting some of these stories together in the same volume seemed to also resemble the queer combination of whiskey and pickles, two things that I acutely enjoy, that seemingly wouldn't fit together, but somehow defy convention and actually do. Therefore, I give you nine of "my children," each unique in its own right, that somehow mesh together to give you a piece of my mind. I hope you love them. T.C.

CHAPTER 1

VICIOUS

I know he really wants to hit me. Maybe stick a fork in my hand again or hit me with another boot. I wish he'd just do and get it over with. Two months and I'll be gone to the military; can't we just wait two damned months? He's standing behind me at the counter, by the telephone. Glaring at the back of my head. All I do is slurp this stupid soup. The gash across my bottom lip hurts like holy hell. He loves it.

"You know the car's totaled? Do you hear me?" he said.

"No I'm fuckin' deaf. I'm three feet away from you for Chrissake." Slow motion.

"Did your grades come?"

"Yeah."

"They came months ago didn't they? Why didn't you show them to us?"

"I threw them away. It was five F's. Is that what you want to know? Five F's. I quit going to school in April when I enlisted. I was out fuckin' off everyday smoking dope and pretending to go to school to make *you* happy. Are you happy?" Where are these tears coming from?

What's he doing? He can't even speak. Just glaring at me like some kinda' maniac. Oh shit, he's going for the drawer, the knives. He's lost it. I'm outta' here. Jeans and a tee shirt. Barefoot. Only a mile to Lisa's house. Slam! He's through the yard. Is he foaming at the mouth? Coming straight at me, with a fuckin' meat cleaver. Faster. He can't catch up.

Lisa and I have known each other since first grade and she is the "nicest" girl I've ever known. Before I knew it wasn't a job, I thought she'd be the Virgin Mary when she grew up. Now when you talk to her, she tries to act all worldly, like everything you say has some hidden dirty meaning. Waiting in her living room makes me wonder why we go out. We have absolutely nothing in common. We'll probably get married. She's been getting changed for a fuckin' hour now. She only lives about a mile away, so I made my great escape here to get a ride to my buddy Ted's house. Her Dad was sitting here when I walked in; I about gave him a coronary. He left the room to take a shit or something. He thinks I'm on dope. He thinks everybody under 50 is on dope. I'm a real charmer when it comes to parents.

"Can you make it to the Better Way meeting with me tomorrow night?" she says.

"Uh, sure I guess so." Like I can say 'no' when she's giving me a ride.

"Good because Joe wants you to do a product demonstration with him. He thinks it'll help you sign some people. I think my Dad asked him."

"Okay, whatever. I'll probably be at Ted's for a while. You think you could pick up some clothes and stuff from my Mom?"

"Sure. I'll go after I drop you off."

Maybe she will be the Virgin Mary.

Staying with Ted is an experience. I ain't picky right now because I don't have many friends to begin with, let alone one with his own place. Be nice if he'd put out some air fresheners or vacuum the shit off the carpet every couple of months though. Smells like toe jam and stale bong water in here. Me, him and his brother Mike grew up together. I'm an only kid so those two are like my brothers, only we actually like each other. Anyway, Ted's a cook at one of the big hotels, and is completely fucking psycho. He goes about 275 and has this long, stringy mop like Meatloaf. I call him that when I'm shit-faced. He fuckin' hates it.

Me, Ted and two other friends are drinking at Peter's Pub, a bar we hang out downtown. Ted gets these nutty ideas sometimes and can let'em go. I told you he's psycho. So, tonight he gets this story going that I'm getting married in the morning and my buddies are taking me out for my bachelor party. He's always trying to get me laid because he thinks I ain't getting no pussy from Lisa. He's right.

"Can I have your attention? Can I have your attention? Hey! Shut the fuck up, I'm tryin' to talk here." It's Ted, drunk as a fuckin' monkey.

"A toast. My buddy's getting married in the morning to Miss Mary Anne Rotten-Crotch of the distinguished Rotten-Crotch brood of East Point. I wish the sorry bastard all the luck in the world...he'll need it."

His scheme works. So well, in fact, I'm getting about 10 rounds of free drinks from people in the bar. I got no shame. We're playing with the story, getting stinkin' ass drunk, when Ted comes back to the table with this gorgeous hard-bodied, black-haired babe. She walks straight up to me, doesn't say a word and rams her tongue half-way down my throat while grabbing two hands full of my ass. I got enough wood in my pants to build a fuckin' canoe.

"Can we sit?"

"You can do whatever you want." She's got to be a pro. Nope. Her friends are too ugly. Besides, I know hookers don't work in groups like that.

"What is the most flattering thing a man can say to a woman?" she asks.

"That she'd make a great president?" I say.

"Good answer."

"So how about you, what's the most flattering thing a woman can say to a man?"

"That she thinks about him when she masturbates."

Wow. All I can say is wow. After about 15 minutes, my eyeballs are bobbin' in my head and I get up to go take a piss. I come back as she's walking out the door alone.

"What the fuck?" I ask Ted.

"What's the matter? Don't you like her?"

"Hell yeah I like her. What's not to like?"

"She asked me if she can go home with you. She wanted to know why you didn't ask her."

"Jesus Christ, she told you that?"

"Yeah. That's why she left. She's waiting outside. If you're not there in 10 minutes she's taking off without you."

"See ya...Ted?"

"Go on, I'll stay at Johnny's tonight. Have fun you lucky bastard."

Luckily I catch her outside and we take a taxi to Ted's apartment. Not two feet in the door she's trying to suck my tongue outta my mouth and unbuttoning my pants. I'm just going with the flow. She's taking rubbers out of her stockings and leading me to the bedroom. What's the hurry? I want to tell her to slow down but I'm afraid she'll stop all together.

"What's your name?"

"Sid."

"I'm Angel. Last night was fun. You okay?"

"I think so."

"Shouldn't you be getting ready for a wedding?"

"Uh, yeah...Angel?"

"What?"

"I don't know what to say. I feel like a dick...The part about the wedding..."

"You mean the part about you made it all up?"

"You knew?"

"Fuck yes. That's an old one. You didn't look the type anyway."

"What'd you mean?"

"You look too pussy hungry. Anyway, I don't do mercy fucks. I fucked you because I felt like it."

"You did?"

"Yeah I did. Why? Does that surprise you?"

"Well, yeah."

"Because I wanted to fuck you or because I admitted it?"

"Both. I mean, I've never been with anyone like you. You're so..."

"Don't be so shallow. And what is 'been with'? Don't you mean fuck? Isn't that how you talk with your buddies?"

"Yeah, but...you're a girl?"

"A girl!? Anyway, don't act. Be yourself. If people can't take it, fuck em."

"I'm sorry about the 'girl' crack. I didn't mean anything."

"Forget it. You're just young."

"What I lack in experience I make up for in enthusiasm."

"So I noticed. Give me your number. Maybe I'll call."

Lisa doesn't ask too much, so I feel kind of obligated when she does. So goes this Better Way business. I was supposed to meet a lot of people and make these great contacts for jobs, but all these people do is talk about selling, selling, selling. If you're not wearing the products, eating the products, shitting the products and wiping your ass with them, they make you feel like a traitor. So I lie and say I am. I think Lisa really is though. She is totally into whatever distracts her for the moment. She is probably making more money in this than her job at the bank. This guy Joe, he's got Better Way on the brain. He's like a triple diamond or something--which means he's raking in the dough. So, Joe's decided to take me under his wing as a favor to Lisa and her Dad. We're going to a meeting tonight of potential converts. I feel like a fuckin' Jehova's Witness or something. Anyway, I'm gonna try. Joe's going to have me do some demos, so after the show the suckers will come to me to sign up. That's where the dough is in this racket. It's not what *you* sell but the percentage you skim off the people who you sign up and what they sell. Very shady dealings here.

So this meeting's going great. Joe could charm the stink off shit. Finally, my turn to do the demo comes. Everything is going along like clockwork--the window cleaner, the dishwashing detergent, the furniture polish--right up the goddamn laundry soap. I get this guy's handkerchief from the crowd and I'm putting shoe polish all over it to show how good the detergent works. It's a nice silk handkerchief and the guy probably honestly shelled about 20-25 bucks for it. Anyway, the idea is I put this filthy old handkerchief in a glass of water, put in a thimble full of soap, swish it around a couple of times, and the hanky comes out spotless. Hurray, hurray.

"Just a few seconds in the water and...well maybe just a few more." This is fucking wonderful. The goddamn hand-kerchief won't come clean. I don't know what's wrong, the material or what. I'm swishing the fuck out of this thing in the glass and nothing's happening. Nothing.

"We must have some pretty hard water around here, huh? Well in that case, we'll just let it soak for a few minutes and come back to it. In the meantime, can I answer any questions about my demonstration?"

"Yeah, can you tell me who's going to replace my handkerchief?"

"It will come clean sir, in just a few minutes."

"What if it don't?"

"Really sir, in just a few more minutes it'll be clean."

"Bullshit. I want my money. It cost me twenty bucks."

"Sir if you'll just..."

"No, you give me my twenty bucks. That stuff don't work!"

"Look you bald-headed senile old fuck, sit your dusty ass down and wait! You'll get your goddamn handkerchief when I'm done with it!"

As can be expected, I put a damper on the evening's festivities. Lisa is totally embarrassed and I honestly couldn't care less. I never wanted to get into this shit in the first place. Being a good sport, she is decent enough to give me a lift back to Ted's.

"Dude, check it out, my brother is coming home." Ted says.

"Great. It'll be good to see him. It's been a while." I say.

"Yeah, look, he's kind of fucked up right now, so be prepared."

"What'd ya mean?"

"Mike's going through this Doors things right now. He thinks Jim Morrison is possessing him. Look, I know it's fucked up. He thought at first he was Jim Morrison reincarnated, then he found out he was born before old Jim died."

"Bummer."

"Yeah. But then he read something about Morrison being possessed by an Indian spirit so he got this other great idea. Since Morrison was dead, maybe he would jump into Mike."

"You're kidding." I say, astonished.

"No man. He took a bunch of acid about two months ago, lit some candles, played 'Riders on the Storm' about twenty times and invited Morrison to use his soul as a place of refuge or some shit."

"You're fuckin' kidding me."

"No. No shit."

"That's fucked up even for Mike."

"Well, there's more. He's writing a play about Morrison and his school's gonna let him put it on in the spring. Since he's Morrison in the play, he's trying to stay in character--all the time."

"What?!"

"When he gets here, just call him Jim."

"Call him Jim?"

"If you call him Mike, he won't answer you."

"Oh Jesus."

"I'm serious. Don't dog him about it or he'll get really pissed."

"This is incredible."

Mike's very artistic and has always been into music and poetry and writing shit down. He's come up with some pretty weird shit, but he's never been possessed by a dead rock star as far as I know.

"So Sidney, how've you been.?" Mike asks.

"Good, uh, *Jim*. How about you?" I reply.

"I've been testing the boundaries of reality to see how far I can go."

"That's cool, Jim. So Ted tells me you're working on a play."

"Yeah, it's like my story. I didn't get to say everything I wanted to last time."

"Cool. You know the other Doors are still around. Maybe you guys could do a reunion tour like The Who, or something, while you're back." I'm trying not to laugh my head off.

"You shouldn't mock what you don't understand."

"Oh fuckin' lighten up Mike it's a joke."

"Sid!" Ted's having a spasm.

"Come on man. Hey, Mike. Yo! Mike, over here dude. Yo! I'm talking to you."

"The problem with you is that you don't recognize the frailness of our existence. Reality is not as certain as you think."

"Reality! Reality is that you're fuckin' mental! Look at you. You can't weigh more than a buck o' five. Your hair's all in your face. You look like shit. You smell like a dead cat. You're stuck in this fucked up hippie-psycho thing."

"Sid, leave him alone. I'm not kidding, lay off. He's working this out."

"Fuck him. He's completely lost his mind. Acid's eaten away too much of his brain."

"I said lay off him. Look man, you'd better go. Chill out and call me later."

"Then fuck you too. You stay here and talk to Jim and find out what the fuck he did with my friend. I'm outta' here."

So now I truly got nowhere to go. When it rains it pours. I don't even know what I'm doing half the time anymore.

I'm tired but I can't sleep. It's pouring down rain and I'm just getting soaked. This really and truly blows dog.

"How'd you find me?" Angel asks.

"Some girl at the bar." I reply sheepishly.

"Why are you here? I told you I'd call you if I wanted to see you."

"I had a problem with Ted. I don't really have anywhere to go. Look, I'm sorry. Maybe this was a bad idea."

"Come in; you're wet. Wait here. I'll get you a towel."

The place is small, like a dorm room. The couch has one of those patch-work quilts and I almost sit on it like a dumb-ass, forgetting I'm soaked to the bone. The kitchen looks real...well, like a normal kitchen. Pots, pans, fridge and stove. I feel weird in here, like I'm going through her personal stuff. Just because I fucked her don't mean we're intimate.

"Dry off with this and I'll put your clothes in the dryer downstairs. Take the brown robe from the bathroom."

There's two of everything in the bathroom. I can't tell if there's any "guy shit" in here because everything looks the same. Toothbrushes, robes, cups, razors. Box of them feminine pad things. There's even plants in here. Who the hell keeps plants in the bathroom? She opens the door. I stand there naked, feeling a little dorky with my python of love shriveled up to about the size of Iggy the Inchworm. Doesn't anybody knock anymore? I hand her my pile of soaked clothes.

"Why don't you take a shower and warm up. I'll be right back."

"Uh, okay. Thanks."

She leaves without another word. The hot water pounds on my back, melting my ice bones. I could stand here all day. I can finally breathe. I catch myself pissing down the drain. Like the piss, I wonder where I'm going.

"Come and sit. I'm making tea. Have you eaten? I'll make sandwiches."

Great. I don't have to talk. She's talking for both of us.

"I have to go out soon. We'll figure out what to do with you when I get back," she says.

The next hour is like some shit you see on Oprah as I tell her about the excitement of my last couple days. My father, my car, college, Lisa, Ted, Mike, Better Way--all the gory details. She's cool for not trying to judge me or give out any free advice. She just listens. I notice she's really good at that. After about two hours she leaves.

What will I do? Nowhere to go and nothing to do when I get there. How did everything get to this point? What a fuck-up I am. "Figure out what we'll do with you" probably means "hasta la vista baby" in a nice way. Why does this shit always happen to me? Why can't I just do what I'm supposed to? Why can't I sleep!? I overcome the temptation to go through all of Angel's stuff while she's gone, not because of my high morals or anything, but because I know she'd find out. That's how my luck works.

"Okay Sid, what are we gonna do with you?" Angel asks.

My mouth doesn't work. My brain won't tell it what to say. All I do is stare at her very serious face. Did you ever notice how different people look when they're being serious? I want to put my face in her lap and cry for a week.

"My roommate's coming home from the hospital in the next few days. You can stay here until then. It's not that I don't want you here...it's just that she's real sick."

"Shouldn't she stay in the hospital until she gets better?"

"She's not going to get better. She's dying. She wants to do it at home where she's comfortable." And she says all of that without so much as flinching. Not a jerk, a pause, a tear or a sigh. She could have been telling me it was a nice day outside or how to tie a shoe.

"Hello."

"Hello, Mom, it's me. I was wondering if..."

"Sid, do you know about Mike?"

"No. I mean, what about Mike?"

"He's in the hospital. He took an overdose of something two nights ago. They don't know if he's going to make it."

I walk all the way from Angel's to the hospital in the rain. About six miles. I don't feel the wet anymore. It runs straight through me. Everything does that lately. I'm not taking the rap for this or feeling guilty, but I feel like I should pay my respects. We've been friends a long time. I'd want him to come and see me. After about two hours I get there. Ted and his Dad are sitting in the hall on a bench like they're bestest buddies. What a crock!

"Sid." Mr. Walters shakes my hand with this lost puppy look.

"Hey Mr. Walters. Hey Ted. Is everything okay?"

"He's still in a coma. Kim and my Mom are in there now. You wanna' go see him?" Ted asks.

"Sure, if it's alright. Ted...I'm..."

"Don't. It's not anybody's fault. Come on, let's go in. They need a break anyhow."

Kim, Mike and Ted's sister, and Mrs. Walters say "hi" and give us tired looks on their way out. If his Mom knew some of the shit we've done she'd have a stroke right here. Mike's got wires and tubes running out of his arm, nose and mouth. He kinda looks like a twisted, skinny little puppet. His eyes are purple and blue, like Rocky during the "Yo Adrian" speech. I want to be closer to him, but not too close. I think he could reach up with one of those puppets arms and grab me. I'd shit myself if he moved right now. Ted's staring with the same look he had in the hallway.

"I found him naked in the tub when I came home from work. A whole bottle of "Jack Black" was empty and his Vicodin stash was lying on the toilet seat, about half gone. The doc said he must have taken about 10 to 15 hits and drank the whole fifth. They pumped his stomach but it was too late."

"Is he gonna be alright?"

"Don't know."

What did I do? I want to tell him that I'm sorry. Sorry for everything. For hitting him in the head with that dirt bomb that cost him four stitches. For putting Exlax in his hot chocolate before we went sleigh riding. For stealing his Cal Ripken rookie card. For putting that big scratch in his Judas Priest CD. I want to tell him that he's always been a brother to me and that I understand. How it's totally fucked up to leave and not say goodbye to your friends. How I know what a dick-head I can be sometimes, but I don't mean nothin' by it.

"You know that's the same way Morrison died? OD'ed in a bathtub in Paris."

"What? What's wrong with you man? That's your brother. Don't you care?"

"Don't you fucking tell me how to feel, asshole. That's right. He's *my brother.* I've been sweating this day for about five years. I'm surprised it took this long or one of us hasn't tried it before."

Fucked up again. Ted's either gonna cry or choke the shit out of me. Mike wants to be left alone. Mr. Walters is coming in because of Ted's yelling. I'm an instant intruder. See ya Mike. Hang tough. Time to go. I've gone enough damage here for one day.

Again I'm walking. The rain's trying to drum a hole through the top of my head. My feet are soaked and the water is squishing through the sides of my Chuck Taylor high tops. I stop and look at the sky. Even God is pissing on me. Where can I go now? Lisa, Ted, Angel, home--nope. I'm not welcome anywhere today. Angel's roommate is coming home. Probably already there. I want to be with somebody but I want to be left alone. I find a doorway.

An idiot stares back from the reflection on the inside of the elevator door. A drowned rat. No, a rat has more; cheese, fleas, other rat friends. You got shit. Everything you touch turns to shit. King Fucking Midas with the shit touch. I hate you. Fuck off, leave, split, take a hike, take a flying fuck at a rolling doughnut, take a flying leap...The elevator bumps to a stop. The doors open and the idiot fades to black.

On the roof I see the dark blanket over the city. It's hollow like me. Over the edge I see wet ants scatter along the sidewalks and wet ant cars wandering lost through the night. A red light from the top of a building a few blocks away winks at me, taunting me. Fuck you too. I'm tired. I dig my smokes out of my jacket and find one not completely soaked. My Zippo, the only reliable part of my whole life right now, doesn't fail me. I suck the smoke deep into my lungs and feel the soothing rush. I walk to the edge and look down. The cold dark concrete doesn't scare me. They say you have a heart attack before you hit. Even if you don't, it happens so fast, that you're dead before you feel the pain. In the sidewalk I see a way out. Relief.

"Going somewhere?"

I almost fall, but catch myself and step back from the ledge. Holding a candle that lights up her face, Angel walks closer.

"You come to save me *Angel*?" I spit.

"Shit, I don't even know if I can save myself. Just do me a favor."

"What?"

"If you're gonna jump, do it off the other side of the building. I don't want the fire department keeping me awake all night scraping your dead ass of the sidewalk."

"Nice to know you care. How'd you know I was here?"

"I saw you come up the street. After you didn't knock I looked around. Wound up here."

"And here I am."

"So here you are." She walks over to the ledge, peeks over and eases away. She doesn't look impressed. "This would do it I'd say. The other side's better though. More traffic."

"Are you trying to get rid of me?"

"I'm not trying to do anything. You're the man. I'm just thinking about my chances of getting a good night's sleep with all the shit you're gonna stir up. Why'd you pick my building anyway?"

"I dunno. This is where I ended up. I didn't want to bother you with Tammy coming home and all."

"She didn't come home."

"No?"

"She died last night."

"I'm sorry..."

"You're getting ready to swan-dive into Barnes Avenue and you're sorry?"

"Well...I..."

"Look, I don't know why I came up here. Maybe I'm just selfish and don't want to lose two friends in two days. But don't feel obligated. Life goes on. I can see now that it's really no big deal. I'm going downstairs. If you decide to take the elevator down, come and see me."

"Wait!"

"What! You want to quit, then quit. Why should I stop you? I won't be here to stop you every time you feel sorry for yourself. I don't need this shit! Go ahead, big man, jump. Jump you fucking loser, *prove* your father right!" She smashes the glass holder and candle at my feet and slams the heavy door to the stairs behind her. The echo booms over the whole roof.

I light another cigarette with my old faithful Zippo. Fuck this shit, I ain't a loser. This whole city can suck my fucking dick before I quit. I flick my smoke down into Barnes Avenue and look at the cold concrete again. This is not my exit. That red fucking light is still winking at me. I wink back and walk to the elevator.

CHAPTER 2
HUNCH

While sitting at the red light, I noticed him walking down the sidewalk. His crisp, new-looking dark blue jeans contrasted with the faded, black, plain t-shirt draped over his razor-lean torso. In his left hand was a jeans-matching insulated metal travel mug, and in his right a mint, black with neon green horizontal stripes, small-sized toolbox. Of the things on him and in his hands, I thought the newness of the toolbox was out of place. It was because of his age. It was hard to estimate his age, because he was older than me, 51, and younger than my dad, 73, but I knew he looked older than he was. It was because of the hunch.

The man's laborious gait seemed as though the Earth's gravitational pull on his body played a mad and gruesome prank on him and was five times as strong, sucking him down into his grave with each pace. It was last that I noticed the man had no teeth. His mouth was closed, his strong jaw taut, but I could tell it was empty. Did he perhaps pick a fight with the wrong gal at the local watering hole and she cleaned his cavities with the fat end of a pool cue? Maybe. Maybe not. That is for a different story at a different time. This story is real.

CHAPTER 3
WHEN THE NIGHT COMES

The Huey beat the air until flight was finally achieved, the craft lifting from the pad. The pilot maneuvered the helicopter skillfully from the small secluded base and over the dense jungle. The call had become a fairly routine transmission. A recon patrol was compromised while conducting surveillance and was now retreating to find a landing zone for quick extraction, the enemy close behind them. The mission of the chopper was to locate the patrol, direct them to a suitable location, and remove them without incident.

It was relatively simple when you thought about it. The copilot navigated, the pilot flew, and the door gunner laid down suppression fire. The major drawback, of course was that they were in a helicopter which was slow, obvious, and easy to hit. As in all conflicts where the helicopter was used, it was considered a major victory by the enemy to disable or destroy it because of the vital mission it performed. With the side door of the airship open, the door gunner scanned the area below in sweeping motions, keeping his finger on the trigger and his watchful gaze bearing down the iron sights of the M-60 machine gun. Within seconds of identifying a hostile enemy target, he could suppress it with a hail of gunfire at a rate of 550 rounds per minute.

"Rich, we should have purple smoke on your side any time now," the pilot spoke to the gunner through the intercom's headset.

"Copy that, sir. I'm lookin'," the gunner replied as he continued the systematic search of the jungle beneath him.

Smoke was used frequently in these situations to mark the landing zone for the choppers. In addition, it allowed the pilot to see the direction and strength of the wind which greatly determined his approach and landing.

"LT, I got smoke. Your nine o'clock, about 2000 meters out," Ellis reported.

"Got it. We're going in. Happy hunting."

The ominous green aircraft banked to the left and began its descent. Ellis scrutinized the area of the smoke as he pulled the gun tightly into his shoulder. He felt himself merge with the weapon and held it tightly, not out of necessity because the gun had virtually no recoil, but out of fondness. He could see the small clearing now. The patrol had wisely placed the smoke on the downwind side of the

LZ, which kept the clearing visible to the pilot. It's going to be a tight fit, Ellis thought. He lifted the sun visor on his helmet and spotted a man from the patrol they were to pick up. It was this man's responsibility to "vector," or guide the helicopter into the LZ. Ellis couldn't see the other members of the patrol; they were probably still inside the tree line maintaining 360-degree security coverage of the area until the chopper had safely landed. The man on the ground held his arms slightly apart in front, palms facing him, and moved his hands repeatedly toward his shoulders, giving the pilot the "move ahead" signal and vectoring the craft into the clearing. Ellis's eyes were wild. They always were at this stage of the mission as he feverishly searched the thick jungle for the enemy.

The pilot reacted to the direction of the signalman, first hovering at a mere five feet, then, slowly descending to the ground. This was the most dangerous time to be in the aircraft. Ellis' heart pounded in anticipation, keeping time with the thumping of the main rotor. Finally, his anxiety was relieved by the sharp cracking of the automatic weapons fire coming from the left front side of the helicopter. The signalman, who had briefly disappeared into the jungle when the skids of the chopper touched the ground, was carrying a man over his shoulders covered in blood. Behind them, three more men quickly retreated toward the chopper, firing sporadically into the thick bush.

Ellis's gun was useless until they lifted off. Too much risk of hitting a friendly. First they had to get all the passengers safely aboard. Ellis quickly unhooked the safety line that connected his harness to the floor of the helicopter so he could assist the men with the wounded. He grabbed the man from the signalman's back, quickly setting him inside on the floor. The signalman followed and administered first aid to the wounded man. Ellis turned as the last three approached the craft and entered. The last soldier threw in his weapon and climbed aboard.

"That's all of us. Let's go," he gasped as he scrambled to aid his buddies.

"That's it, let's fly!" Ellis shouted into the intercom, as he grabbed the gun, swiveling it on its pedestal to greet the now advancing enemy. He looked up from the gun just in time to see an enemy soldier scamper to the edge of the clearing. Ellis turned the M-60 on him and unleashed a fifteen-round burst directly into the man's chest, causing him to execute a dramatic back flip before crumbling to the ground. He heard the loud dings of enemy rounds as they penetrated the helo's metal skin. One round entered a soldier's leg, and upon exiting, burst in a fine red mist.

As the Huey started to slowly lift and hover, Ellis dumped a barrage of gunfire, saturating the jungle tree line. The Huey climbed slowly. Two, four, six feet. Ellis saw movement from what appeared to be a dozen men advancing toward the clearing. Eight, ten, twelve feet and still climbing. Soon they would be high enough to move forward. Ellis steadily poured destruction on everything he saw moving.

"This is gettin' terminal in a ..." Ellis began, but was quickly cut off by a bright flash that caught his attention from the thick tree line. A large explosion shuddered the Huey as a rocket-propelled grenade tore into the tail section, severing the tail-rotor drive shaft. With the aircraft only hovering, and the tail rotor unable to function, the craft was now made unstable by the momentum of the main rotor. The gunship spun wildly in a counter-clockwise direction.

Confined to the small clearing without ample altitude to escape, it took only seconds for the tail section to hit a large tree, the force throwing Ellis from the craft to the jungle below. Before anyone inside the helicopter realized what happened, a second rocket found the fuel bladder, aft of the crew compartment. The Huey, engulfed in a swirl of flames, slowly descended into the clearing.

Ellis returned to consciousness with a piercing pain in his left shoulder. As he tried to move his arm, the fire intensified in his neck. He gingerly placed his right hand on the injury and confirmed his fear; broken collarbone. Through the inky darkness he assessed his predicament. The blank cement walls with a small rectangular window, rusty iron bars on three sides, and a damp dirt floor, told him he was positively not among friends. His next sensation was the overpowering odor of urine that burned his nostrils. Next, the heat. It made the fragrance all the more unappealing. No, Dorothy, he thought, we're sure as hell not in Kansas anymore. It finally came back to him. The crash. For better or worse, he had survived. In the darkness on the other side of the bars, he detected movement. A dark shadow approached.

"Hey, you okay?" it whispered.

"I...think so. Where...?" he started.

"Prison camp. Somewhere in Crow Valley. The old RPA bravo compound I think." The "old" Philippine Army compound was right. It was one of the first sites that fell at the beginning of the escalated conflict.

"How long have I been here?

"The dinks brought you in sometime in the late morning," he said referring to their Filipino adversaries.

"Who runs this hell hole?" Ellis said as he struggled to a sitting position.

"NPA all the way. A renegade Army outfit had it for a while, but lost it. There's a bunch of RP army regulars in with us, too. How'd you wind up here?"

"Chopper crashed on a recon extract just south of hill 338. Anybody else come in here with me?"

"No, just you."

Ellis said nothing else, realizing he was the only one who had survived. After a brief moment for respect, he and the nebulous figure, who he learned was an Air Force F-16 pilot named Kent, traded stories about what they'd heard about the U.S. military's current "police action" in the Republic of the Philippines. The overthrow of the "elected" government had been a matter of perfect timing. Four months after the American forces had been pulled out, the island of Mindanao decided to secede from the rest of the country. The NPA, New People's Army, had somehow managed to organize and unify, and a power-hungry faction of the Philippine Armed Forces had decided to revolt. The government could withstand one of these actions on its own; however, with the combination of all three, it took less than a week for the Manila government to crumble. And so was born the Coup-of-the-Month Club. The secession and military coup wasn't what bothered the U.S. It was the propaganda that the NPA were true red-blooded commies that got them involved. Ellis didn't care much about the circumstances. A puppet government in exile was functioning in Baugio City, high in the northern mountains of Luzon. Six months into the conflict, there seemed to be no swift end in sight.

"Can you walk?" Kent inquired.

"I think so."

"Listen, there's been talk about an escape. Seems one of the locals has some bargaining power with one of the guards. He figures if he helps us, we'll take him back to the world. You know the States, the big BX."

31

"Not interested," Ellis replied flatly. "The time's not right."

He felt around in the dark, finding only a small pot, the source of the intriguing aroma. Finding nothing suitable to use for bedding, he eased himself to the earthen floor and quickly fell asleep in a sliver of moonlight pouring through the small window.

"Gising na!" the guard shouted for the men to get up, jolting Ellis from his sleep. The only lighting in the facility came from the small window in each cell. In the improved lighting, Ellis could see that there were six cells in the building but only three occupants: himself, Kent, and a man wearing a uniform showing that he had once been in the Philippine Air Force. The guard confidently strolled from cell to cell, tapping the bars with a two-foot long piece of sturdy bamboo. He stopped at Ellis' cell which was second from the entrance.

"Hey, Joe, did you sleep good?" he taunted.

The guard was dressed in well-worn, three-sizes-too big-green jungle fatigues, a feeble attempt at a mustache and beard sprouting from his face. Ellis sat silently in the far corner of his cell, staring blankly at the man. Next door, Kent approached the front of the cage.

"This GI is very sick. He needs a doctor," he offered, searching for a hint of compassion in his foe.

"No doctor here for you. You going to die on me Joe?"

"I'll survive," Ellis returned.

"We will see."

Shortly after the guard made his check, a young boy, clad in rags, served them lunch, which consisted of cold rice and a piece of casaba root on a banana leaf. The youth did not make eye contact with anyone in the cages.

"That boy's part of our escape plan," Kent told him. "He's got no family left except a sick mother."

Ellis wolfed the meal down. He had to keep his strength and was uncertain when the next meal would be. The day passed without incident and Kent rambled on about what he'd do with his freedom. Ellis tried to stretch and keep himself occupied with moderate exercise while awaiting the night. Though his injury was extremely painful, he was confident it would be completely healed in a few days. The moon, nearly full, rose slowly outside his window. He settled in a corner, trying to get comfortable, waiting for sleep to come.

"Have you thought about your plan for getting out of here?" Kent whispered.

"Yeah."

"Well?"

"Soon," he answered, and slowly drifted off to sleep.

Morning was once again initiated with an attendance check by Mr. Hospitality.

"Is he always so pleasant?" Ellis asked Kent when the guard had finally departed.

"Flores isn't so bad. As a matter of fact, he's part of the plan too."

"How so?" Ellis moved closer to the bars that divided his and Kent's cells.

"He makes two head counts a day. One in the morning, and one around midnight after everybody's asleep. His shift runs from midnight to eight in the morning. Other than his checks, the only other person who has contact with us is the dink who checks in the early afternoon, and Rigo, the boy who brings the chow."

'And you already said he's in on it."

"Yeah but I'm not sure exactly how. See, there used to be a Philippine Air Force captain in the cell next to yours. Name was Reyes. He and that other Filipino at the other end of the block, Perez, came in here together. Those two originally came up with the plan.

"What happened to Reyes?"

"Not sure. He had a touch of malaria when they brought him in. One night he started convulsing. We called for

Flores and he came and took him away. That was about four days ago. We haven't heard about him since."

"What about Flores? I thought he was part of the plan."

"He said they sent Reyes up to Camp O'Donnell to see the doc. We don't completely trust Flores but he's all we got. They've only been keeping prisoners here for about three months. You and me are the only Americans I know about. Perez has been taking care of all the escape details. All I know is that there's finally a way out of here and I'm taking it."

"When is this big plan supposed to happen?"

"We're waiting on Flores. Are you in?"

"Tell me more."

The plan was simple. The guard, Flores, would come to escort them to see the Camp Commander. He would come sometime before midnight, which was shift change for all of the guards. The only people working at night in the camp were the four tower guards and about a dozen men who randomly patrolled inside and outside of the compound. By removing the prisoners before shift change, the oncoming guards would not notice them missing. Since Flores was the only one who performed the head counts, no one would discover their disappearance until he failed to report for shift change in the morning. Flores regularly had business at Camp O'Donnell, which was serving as a regional NPA stronghold about twenty miles away, so no one would question his departure in the middle of the night. The plan was to place the prisoners in a covered, two and a half-ton truck, which would be parked next to the Camp Commander's office, then exit the camp. Kent wasn't sure what Perez had worked out with Flores or where Rigo came in; he only knew that Perez and Reyes had wanted him to get them to America.

Kent informed Perez that he wouldn't go unless they took Ellis with them. He agreed that two Americans would be more help than one. When Rigo brought the daily meal, Perez conversed briefly with him in Tagalog, then told the men they should get ready to go tonight. The men sat silently for the remainder of the day, each scripting his own fantasy of freedom. Night came on them slowly, accompanied by a full moon.

Ellis stood dreamily in front of his window, bathing in the moonlight. He thought of his family. He carried on his heritage proudly, like his father before him. There had been great warriors in the Ellis clan for several generations. Theirs was a family steeped in tradition...and mystery. He remembered the secret every time the pale, silvery moon rose fully in the sky. He always fought the urge to change at these times and was grateful that the change could only come by his own free will. It hadn't always been this way; his grandfather had told him. Many generations before, the Ellis men had no control over their secret, and as a result, many had to be destroyed. Rich Ellis was thankful that evolution had favored him.

The prisoners were stirred from their thoughts as Flores made his entrance. It was time to go. Flores and two other guards carrying M-16s took them from their cells and proceeded directly to the truck. The prisoners climbed into the back and sat on the floor, well concealed from outside observation. The three guards sat up front.

"Too bad that Reyes couldn't be with us," Kent said breaking the long silence.

"He has already been freed," Perez stated evenly.

"But I thought...I mean...he was so sick."

"This is how it appeared. Flores said he would not free us unless he received the money first. To do this, Reyes faked an illness so he could be transported to the medical facility at Camp O'Donnell. On the way, Flores let him go to make arrangements with his brother to gather the money from his family and mine. His brother was then to take the money to Rigo's house. As soon as Rigo received it, he would inform Flores and he would take us out. The bargain was that we must be out before Rigo gives him the money. Rigo must have gotten the money today."

The truck came to a halt. They heard the doors open and close. As they sat up in the back of the truck, they saw the other two guards posted on both sides of the tailgate. Beyond the guards, they saw Flores standing at the edge of the road, looking across a darkened field. A figure approached him -- Rigo. After a short conversation, too low for the prisoners to make out, Rigo handed him a package wrapped in a burlap sack. Flores casually drew a pistol from the holster on his hip and fired one shot into the boy's forehead. Rigo collapsed in a heap.

They might have stared at the dead boy forever, but for the sounds they suddenly heard. Sounds of cracking bones. Kent's gaze frantically searched for the noise and saw Perez sitting next to him, an equally puzzled look on his face. He did not see Ellis. He must have moved to the front of the truck bed, where the strange sounds were coming from.

"Ellis, are you okay?" he slid towards him.

"Stay back!" a deep and distorted voice, which faintly resembled Ellis' spoke. Kent froze. Whatever made that sound wanted its privacy far more than he wanted to investigate.

Flores appeared at the tailgate, startling them.

"Captain Reyes was good enough to send my money. He bought his freedom for now. I cannot afford your escape on my record. I also cannot risk you telling anyone about our plan. We will take your bodies back to camp. We caught you trying to escape. Me and my men will be heroes. I am sure of the boy's silence." The succinct pronunciation of English, typical among Filipinos in the habit of being around Americans, was particularly unnerving what it announced their death sentence. The guards unhooked the latch on the heavy tailgate and pulled it open, their weapons fixed on the men.

"Salabas!" he motioned for the men to disembark. As Kent started to move, he was pushed back against the side of the bed by a dark figure that blurred past him, catching Flores full in the throat. The hairy figure was an explosion of deft movement as it literally tore the man limb from limb. After the other two guards recovered from their initial shock, they pointed their weapons at the figure and released a long volley of automatic fire. The figure was unaffected. It reared up on its hind legs in front of the guard closest to him, and made one powerful, neck-level sweep, severing his head. Its preternatural quickness was devastating. The second guard threw his rifle to the ground and ran with arms and legs flailing in disjointed, wild movements. The figure pounced on the guard's back as its powerful jaws clamped the base of his skull, then quickly withdrew.

Kent and Perez remained motionless in the truck, fearing the worst. Their eyes moved quickly about the massacre outside the truck, but detected no movement. Then seeming to materialize from the night, Ellis reappeared. It took Kent more than a moment to realize Ellis wore no clothes, but was splattered with blood down his right arm, all over his mouth, and down the front of his neck to mid-chest.

All three men were silent as Ellis climbed into the truck and quickly dressed. He wiped the blood away the best he could with his t-shirt. Perez jumped out of the truck and recovered the dead men's weapons. When Ellis finished dressing, he also got out of the vehicle. He made several large circles with his left arm, pleased with his newly healed collarbone.

"Perez, I think you should drive in case we get stopped. Kent and I will stay out of sight in the back, to avoid attention."

The other men did not move, staring blankly at Ellis.

"Let's move out fellas. This is no night to be out. There's a bad moon on the rise."

CHAPTER 4
AN IMMODEST PROPOSAL

"Worthington Distributors. Mary Burke speaking. May I help you?"

"Yes, madam, I believe you can."

"Steven! What a surprise! Are you back?"

"Yes, I just got in. How's about dinner at seven? Fancy dress. Tonight it's on me. I'll even pick you up for a change. Whaddaya say?"

"Well...okay. Sure. Seven will be fine. Steven, is anything wrong?"

"Wrong? No, everything is right as rain. Better than ever."

"All right. See you at seven then. I love you."

"Uh-huh, bye."

$$\mathbin{\text{━━+ +━━}}$$

"Hello."

"Hello, Mother. I won't be home for dinner tonight. Steven is back from Boston and he wants to take me out."

"Is everything alright dear? You don't sound yourself. Did he say something to upset you?"

"I don't know. Something has changed. He sounded so different on the phone. So...decisive. This isn't like him."

"You've know each other for so long. I'm sure if there was a problem, you would have seen it coming."

"I'm not sure. He's been traveling so much and putting so many hours in at work. We haven't seen a lot of each other lately."

"Don't worry dear. Whatever's happening, you'll know soon enough. I'll see you when you come home to change for your date. I love you."

"I love you, Mother. Bye."

$$\mathbin{\text{━━+ +━━}}$$

"Cassini's. May I help you?"

"Yes, I'd like to make a reservation for two for dinner. Tonight. Seven-thirty. Name is Adams. Steven Adams."

"Very good Mr. Adams. Is there anything else I can help you with?"

"Yes, I'd like a table by the fire. And I was hoping you could do me a service. I'd like to reserve violins to coincide with our after-dinner drinks. I'm also having flowers delivered at six sharp and would like to have them brought to the table when the music starts. You see, I'm going to propose marriage tonight."

"I will handle all of the arrangements myself. Congratulations Mr. Adams."

"Yes."

━━◁┼ ┼▷━━

"Images Beauty Salon. Rosalind speaking. May I help you?"

"Hi Roz, this is Mary Burke. Can you squeeze me in today?"

"Hi Mary. Well, I'm booked through five. Let me see what I can do. What's the rush at the last minute?"

"My Steven just came back from a business trip and he wants to go out to dinner. I'd feel better with a fresh look. Maybe a trim and a set?"

"Well, if it's in the name of love I don't see how I can say no. If you can make it by one, I can squeeze you in."

"Thanks Roz. You're a life saver."

"See you then."

⊷ ⊶

"King's Ransom Jewelers."

"May I speak to Ben Edwards?"

"This is Ben Edwards."

"Ben, Steven Adams of Centurion Alarm Sales. How've you been?"

"Hi Steven. Business is well."

"How's your system doing?"

"Worth its weight in gold. I'm very happy with it."

"Glad to hear that. Hey, the reason I'm calling is to ask about something in that catalogue you gave me the last time I was in."

"Sure, you got the page number?"

"Yes, 33, bottom left-hand side. Item G-54. Do you have that in?"

"It's one full carat. Diamond solitaire engagement ring. Yep I got it. What size do you need?"

"Six should do it, but you can always resize it, right?"

"Absolutely."

"What's that one go for?"

"Let me see...I'll give you 20% off. Brings it down to 18 hundred even. Preferred customer price."

"I'll take it. Ben, you're a pal. Can I pick it up today? Say about five?"

"Sure. Who's the lucky gal?"

"Miss Mary Burke of the Severna Park Burke's. And you got that right. She's the luckiest girl in the world to land a catch like me."

"All that class and modest too. See you at five then Steven."

"See you then."

≕ ≔

"Good afternoon, Gateway Travel, Fran Michaels, can I help you?"

"Hi Fran, it's Mary. Are you busy?"

"Hi Mary. No, it's slow as mud here. How are you?"

"I'm not sure. Has Jacob said anything to you about Steven lately? Anything I should know about?"

"Well, no. Why do you ask?"

"Steven just got back from a business trip from Boston this morning and he asked me out to dinner. It's not like him to be so unpredictable, you know, so off the cuff. I thought something was wrong and Jacob would know if anyone would."

"I'm sure if Jacob knew something he'd tell me. You know what a blabber mouth he is. What do you think could be wrong?"

"Maybe...I don't know Fran. It's just that we've been dating for so long. Eight years now, on and off. Maybe's he's grown tired of me. I used to think we'd get married, but Steven always refuses to talk about it until he's more financially secure. I've always thought it was an excuse to put me off."

"How can you think that? Steven has never been with anyone else. You've know each other since we were in high school. I'm sure he's just being cautious. You know how he is."

"I just don't know what I'd do without him. I can't bear to think of it. He's my whole life."

"Nonsense! Mary, listen to yourself. You sound like a pitiful old maid."

"Isn't that I've become? Isn't it the truth?"

"No, it's not! You are a pretty, talented and brilliant woman. You'd be a great catch for anyone. Thirty is not old. Now pull yourself together and go to dinner. Whatever happens you'll be fine. And if you ask me, you're not the one who needs Steven. It's Steven who needs you. He can't live with his parents forever. He's a 30-year-old man."

"I don't know. Maybe I'm making too much of this. He seemed so different on the phone. I think he's going to break it off."

"Well if he does, it's his loss. I'm here for you."

"Thanks Frannie. I've got to run. Talk to you later."

Cassini's possessed a magical quality that Steven had not remembered during his previous visits, which were the second Saturday of each month, Valentine's Day, Mother's Day, and his and Mary Ann Burke's birthdays. It was his favorite place to eat, not so much because he loved the food or the atmosphere, which were never lacking; he liked Cassini's because the staff made him feel like somebody. All of the employees knew Steven by name and greeted him politely upon each and every visit.

The table by the fireplace was indeed the table of his dreams. The table that he knew that one night he would propose to his future wife. Tonight was that night. They had just finished their meal. Veal parmesan, Caesar's salads, sides of fettuccini, bread sticks, and house wine. Steven liked things to be steady, reliable, and dependable, without change. This is why Mary was so startled at his suggestion of this dinner. It was against his routine.

Their conversation, from the time Steven picked her up at her mother's house, through the main course and dessert, had been the usual mindless chatter Mary had grown accustomed to, but never actually bothered her until tonight. He talked about his day and his business trip and his opinions. Just for amusement, during the tiramisu, Mary counted the number of times he said I, me, or my. Forty-four. Through dessert alone. She wondered what he could possibly do besides sales. He never shut up. Did he stop to breathe? Was he human? She had always accepted what she considered to be her biggest drawback: she was plain. She has a plain face, plain figure, and plain hair. She considered herself lucky to have a man. Any man. Her father told her that often, right up to his death three years ago. Steven Adams was captain of the tennis team in high school and college, top salesman for Centurion Alarm Sales, and headed for management. She could do worse. This is how she felt her whole life, as far back as she could remember, right up to before this very moment.

"Mary Ann, I've got something very important to say to you. All of the long hours and travelling have paid off. When I went to the corporate office in Boston, I met with the big boys. They are very impressed with me. They want to make me assistant district manager. Isn't that wonderful?"

"Yes, Steven. It's wonderful. Your parents must be very proud."

In her mind a switch was turned. Sudden and definite. She felt as though she were in a coma yet still somehow able to speak. She felt nothing. Out of the corner of her eye she noticed the waiter bringing flowers.

"That's not the best of it. I get a company car, a huge expense account, a bonus, my own parking spot, and a 25 thousand a year raise!"

She forced a smile. She never minded his climb to the top. She only now felt like each time he climbed, he used her head as a step. She thought he liked to have her around because she made him feel not so plain by comparison. Yes, that had to be it. Well, ain't that a kick in the...

"Of course you know what this means. I'll finally be financially secure enough to make you an honest woman."

She stared at him blankly. She faintly heard violins playing a heart-wrenching Italian love song. This schlep wasn't dumping her. He was going to propose! Her lips parted slightly. She still stared, but now in utter disbelief. This was going to be good, she thought.

"Well, here goes. I've already put a deposit on quaint little townhouse over in Hillsdale and told my folks *your* good news. I've decided April 23rd is the day. Now you can just call the church, send out invites and we'll make it official. I've got dates held for a week in Aruba for our honeymoon. Before you know it, it'll be you and me and baby makes three."

He opened the small felt covered box in the palm of his hand, exposing the glittering diamond ring. She was speechless and numb. Without blinking, she raised her gaze to meet his and softly spoke the first syllables she had ever uttered to him which vaguely resembled defiance.

"Are you proposing or informing?"

"Excuse me?"

"I said are you proposing marriage to me or informing me of your plans?"

"What do you mean?!"

"I mean that I'm tired of being talked at instead of talked to. I'm not your puppy! I've had it!"

"Mary Ann, you don't know what you're saying!"

That was partially true because she felt as though she were only along for the ride with someone else at the controls of her mind. Although unsure of the origins of the words she spoke, she liked them and became very amused. Quickly standing, she realized how loud she had been speaking the last few moments. She snatched her purse from the empty chair.

"Steven you are plain and you bore me. You... you can suck it!"

She crossed the dining room and walked through the door into the cool night air, never feeling so free and alive.

CHAPTER 5
LOST IN TIME

The elevator ride was shakier than usual this morning. The carriage felt like it was sticking to the side of the chute as it jerked upward. After coming to an abrupt halt at the thirty-third floor, he exited and crossed the poorly-lit hallway to the dark, faux wood, perma-plastic door to his office. As he opened the door, the violence of the bright orange carpet to his ultra-sensitive, vodka-soaked eyeballs, made him cringe from the added insult to his hangover. Ophelia, his doting secretary, sat pertly and dutifully at her desk, typing a background investigation on her terminal. She wore a conservative but elegant golden blouse over a modest-length, rust-colored skirt, which complimented the burgundy shade of her jaw length bob and emerald eyes.

"Good morning Ophelia," he groaned.

"Good morning Mr. Hansing" she returned, looking up from her terminal, then respectfully averting her eyes as to not to seem to be reproaching him for another night of excesses.

"Anything interesting happen over the night?"

"No sir, but there is a priority message for you to contact Elmont Jarvis at your first opportunity. Would you like me to connect you?"

"Yeah, give me five. Do we have anything for a headache?" he asked as he wobbled to his office.

He felt more confident once in the stability of his own chair. Ophelia brought a small medicine bottle and a bottle of water and set them on the desk. He fumbled with the childproof cap, until Ophelia took the bottle from him, deftly depressed and released the top and dropped two tablets in his hand.

"Better make it three," he said. She dropped another one in his palm and gave him a motherly smile, which he didn't notice.

"Ophelia, how would you feel about an emotional upgrade and the addition of a few…comfort options?" he squirmed with the last words. She looked at him with what appeared to him to be a look of surprise, until he realized that was an impossible emotion with her current emotional configuration.

"Are you displeased with my performance as your secretary Mr. Hansing?" she seemed to frown, also impossible. It was fairly common for owners, when they wanted to upgrade their "office equipment," to buy the latest secretarial model, to reconfigure the old model to a pleasure unit. People got attached to cyborgs after a while, whether as a matter of sentimentality or by simply forgetting that they were part machine. Ophelia thought she was being demoted.

"Not at all. It's just that I was thinking that…that maybe I could use you as a constant companion instead of just here at the office," he responded exasperated.

"If you are proposing that you want me to fulfill the function of a human wife," she replied, "I think that would be a wonderful idea. Of course, if that is what you desire, sir."

He could have sworn he saw her smirk. Of course that wasn't possible. There was something very peculiar about the way her mental implant had chosen the words "proposing" and "wife" in the same sentence.

"Well…then…great," he stammered, "I just wanted to know how *you* felt about it. Uh…could you get me through to Mr. Jarvis now?"

"Right away, sir." There it was again. He could have sworn he saw her smile.

⇥⇤ ⇥⇤

The videophone terminal on the right side of Hansing's desk flashed the face of Jarvis's secretary, a base model-business cyborg named Rita, who lacked any of Ophelia's appealing physical upgrades. Her mousy brown hair pulled into a bun at the back of her head reminded Hansing of the talking heads used in primary education. Her faced remained pale and expressionless. Not like Ophelia at all.

"Mr. Jarvis will be with you momentarily Mr. Hansing." Rita spoke.

"Thank you." Hansing thought that Jarvis must keep Rita for sentimental reasons. With his kind of resources Hansing was sure he could afford the top of the line models or maybe even a, heaven forbid, a human secretary. They did still exist for those with the resources to afford them, but it was a rarity.

"Mr. Jarvis…" Rita said as she announced Jarvis' face to the terminal. Jarvis had one of those fortunate faces that seemed to get more distinguished with age. Hansing saw it as a face that didn't see much work and the stress that goes with having a "real" job, with his oily, jet-black hair, silvered at the temples, with a tan that he believed may be from actual, real sun. "Wow," he thought, "this guy must really be loaded." Complementing the face was a fresh manicure and a dark gray mohair suit. Mohair was the new cashmere, which was the old wool, which was now the new denim. Hansing got so distracted by his initial impression that he nearly missed Jarvis' eyes. Dark circles. Red. Been crying?

"Mr. Hansing I'll be straight and clear. My wife is missing," Jarvis said firmly. He'd been drinking.

"For how long?" Hansing asked, less firmly, and more compassionately.

"She went to her sector, Tyrill, two weeks ago for a one-week trip. I spoke to her last week, prior to her return, and everything appeared to be in order."

"What day was she due back here on Earth?"

"Three days ago. When she didn't arrive as planned, I was concerned. After speaking with her family and the travel agent, we found out that she departed transport but didn't arrive here. Something…terrible…," he began to lose himself, but recovered, "Mr. Hansing can you help me? I… please…can you?"

"Mr. Jarvis, I can only begin to understand your fear, but why have you contacted me? Why don't you try a travel engineer to investigate this for you? This seems like a technical issue. I have no scientific background in time travel. In fact, I dread it." Hansing didn't like the direction this conversation was going. As he said, this type of travel, long distance, interplanetary travel, involved time travel, and that was just one of the marvels of new science that he could not get used to.

"I tried them. All of them. Useless. All of them. I was told she just disappeared during travel. Poof. Snatched during the trip. A glitch. Mr. Hansing, I am a very wealthy and powerful man. I would not rule out the possibility of kidnapping. There is something criminal, maybe even sinister going on here. Law Enforcement came and took a report and said it was beyond their scope. I need you to ensure my wife is safely returned to me. I am told you get things done. That you solve problems."

Something in the pit of Hansing's stomach turned into a shaky bowl of gelatin. He wanted to tell Jarvis that no, he couldn't help him and to forget it. Then he remembered the reason he became a private investigator: to help people, to take the cases the cops wouldn't take, to rescue damsels, to help when no one else would. He already knew the cops couldn't help with anything like this. They contract missing person's cases to PI's, and since Jarvis wouldn't have a choice in who worked the case, he was better coming directly to someone of his own choosing.

"Mr. Jarvis, I will take your case. I make you no promises other than I will do my best...."

"Thank –"

"Don't thank me until you hear me out. There is only one way I do things when I'm working a case, and that's my way. I'll hear you out, but all decisions are mine. It's your money, but I am taking all of the risks."

"I'll pay you any –"

"My fee will be fair and reasonable, but the expenses will be ridiculous and I need advances for expenses. I don't have the kind of working capital for this. Anyway, give my secretary access to your files on Mrs. Jarvis, and we'll do the contract. Once you accept my terms, I'll get started."

"Thank you Mr. Hansing. As you say. My secretary will contact yours straight away." The monitor went black.

"Ophelia?" Hansing spoke and the voice-activated monitor brought Ophelia's face onscreen.

"Yes sir?"

"Please assign Mr. Jarvis a case number under missing persons, direct billing. His secretary will be sending you access for their files. I'll need them as soon as possible, today. Also, I'll need an appointment with our travel agent and controller. I'm going to the Tyrillean sector. Standard arrangements while I'm gone"

"Yes sir. Anything else?"

"Yes. Actually…" he started nervously, "contact Panterra Cyborgenetic Research Center. Get a cost estimate and installment time on those upgrades we discussed. Use your judgment on the options and what we can afford. That's it. Thanks. End." He ended the call quickly, with the voice action, because he didn't want her to see the embarrassing redness in his face. Cyborgs were part human and part machine. Ophelia had a human heart and some of her other organs.

Her brain was human but had been damaged in a vehicle accident when she was 29 years old, and was augmented my implants. Her arms were replaced as a result of the accident but she still had her natural, beautiful, long, legs...

The Sandor Travel Agency occupied an ultra-modern ten-story structure in the center of the city. It had the reputation of being the best, which is probably why Mr. Jarvis used it to send his beautiful wife Rachel on her vacation. It was a bit expensive for Hansing's usual expense account but since Mrs. Jarvis departed from here and since Mr. Jarvis was picking up the tab, it seemed the natural place to start. The receptionist on the first floor directed him to Intergalactic Travel Arrangements on the ninth floor. He approached the reception area and was greeted by a smartly dressed blonde receptionist.

"May I help you, sir?" She asked.

"My name is Vicman Hansing, I believe my secretary set up a ten o'clock appointment for me." He couldn't be positive but he was quite sure nearly everyone in the building was a cyborg or robot. It was not uncommon for this kind of business.

"Yes sir, Mr. London is expecting you," she replied. That made him feel a little better. Mr. London was probably human. Most non-humans don't use titles in front of their names. That helps easily fooled humans distinguish "man from machine." The receptionist directed him into Mr. London's office. The room was all white and highly polished chrome. The man whom Hansing presumed to be Mr. London sat behind a large glass top desk. He directed him to sit on the long white couch directly in front of it.

"How can I help you Mr. Hansing?" he began the conversation.

"I'm a private investigator researching the disappearance of Mrs. Rachel Jarvis," Hansing said. "I would like to review her file and speak to her controller if possible. I will also be needing travel to the Tyrillean Sector."

"Elmont Jarvis is one of our best and most treasured clients. I will do everything in my power to assist you. Virgil was Rachel's controller during her travel. I will have him join us at once."

Mr. London was dressed in a conservative black business suit which accented his blond hair and pale features. He appeared to be in his early thirties and from his mannerisms he was definitely human. He pushed a single button on a large console on his left. Moments later a man nearly identical in appearance to Mr. London entered the room.

"Virgil, this is Mr. Hansing. He needs some information regarding the recent travel arrangements of Mrs. Rachel Jarvis. Mr. Hansing this is Virgil. He should be able to supply you with all of the information you will need. If you will excuse me, I will see personally to your travel arrangements to the Tyrillean Sector." Mr. London departed through a side door and Virgil seated himself on the couch next to

Hansing. Simply by the absence of any physical documentation regarding the Jarvis file to prompt him, he knew Virgil was a synthetic.

"Mr. Jarvis' secretary Rita contacted our agency sixteen days ago on the 14th of November and requested travel arrangements to Ty Per, the second planet from the sun in the Tyrillean Sector. Rita stated that Mrs. Jarvis would be travelling alone and would be in Ty Per for eight days. Her nature of travel would be pleasure. On the 24th of November at 4:00 pm Earth time zone 5, she would be on return travel, terminating at Earth."

"Virgil, could you explain the process of her trip in laymen's terms to me?" Hansing asked. Since he only had a slight concept of intergalactic travel, this was difficult for him to fathom.

"Yes sir. Mrs. Jarvis was placed in our molecular disassembly chamber and her entire physical body was broken down to the molecular level. Then the molecules were projected through cosmic strings at ultralight speed to Ty Per, arriving in the future, the time required for travel, then once in the closed-loop time compensator at Ty Per, which actually sent her back into time, proportionate to the travel time, she actually arrived in Ty Per the exact time that she departed Earth, which was at 9:00 am on the 16th of November. Since her stay in Ty Per was only for a short period of time, I monitored her for the duration of her stay, assisted by controller Sheena in Ty Per. Then on the 24th of November at 4:00 pm, she entered the departure terminal on Ty Per and the travel attendants projected her toward Earth. She would have entered Earth's closed-loop time compensator, due to the travel time in the future, then circled it until present time was established, but she never arrived at the terminal here on Earth on the 24th. She has not been located as of the present," Virgil concluded with computer-like precision. He expressed absolutely no emotion in his details of the account, which didn't really surprise Hansing, considering what Virgil was programmed to do. While Virgil's explanation of long distance travel sunk in, Mr. London returned and informed Hansing that his travel arrangements were prepared and that he could go whenever he was ready. Hansing asked Mr. London to have his secretary notify Ophelia of his departure and he proceeded to the departure terminal.

The terminal was decorated in the same white and chrome pattern of Mr. London's office. There was a large waiting area in the center of the open space, with the familiar long couches. Against the far wall were twelve chambers, each with a single white windowless door and its respective number. Off to the side of the room were the controller's terminals, also numbered one to twelve, where a dozen cyborgs were seated in front of large monitors. Virgil was at number nine, Mr. London standing over his shoulder and making the final preparations for Hansing's trip. Mr. London approached him and asked him to be seated.

"Mr. Hansing, are you prepared for your journey?" Mr. London asked.

"As prepared as I'm going to be," Hansing answered, his mouth dry and palms sweating. He was not thrilled with his impending travel.

"Have you ever travelled long distance before?"

"Yes, in the military when I was younger. Back and forth to Campbell Sector. It was a long time ago and I haven't travelled since."

"There's no need to worry, Virgil is our best controller. He will monitor you throughout your trip. Will two days be long enough for your business?"

"Should give me enough time to find out what I need to. I will report to the Ty Per departure terminal on December third."

"Please proceed to Chamber nine Mr. Hansing," Virgil interrupted. Hansing took his briefcase and walked to the door marked "9." Inside he found a mattress on a platform, covered by a glass dome, which was pulled away from the bed.

"Mr. Hansing, please lie down on the bed and place your briefcase on your chest. Keep all parts of your body inside the dome, on the mattress." Virgil instructed. Hansing did as he was told. The glass dome slowly lowered over him and locked in place with a muffled "click." The last thing he remembered was a faint mist surrounding his head and getting very sleepy.

Hansing awoke in what seemed like only minutes, in an identical domed bed, with a strong taste of walnuts in his mouth. It was the same walnut aftertaste he had never gotten used to while travelling with the Colonial Marines. It was the only side effect that he was aware of from time travel. The glass dome unlocked and slowly raised. A soft, feminine voice filled the dome, telling Hansing to gather his belongings, depart the chamber, and proceed to the controller terminal. Sitting at the terminals were one cyborg each. They looked different from the one that he left on Earth. All of these had the physical attributes of Tyrilleans: brown complexions, reddish –brown eyes, and a hair that appeared to be black but was also a very dark red when lighted. The controller at terminal nine was a female with shoulder-length hair, and like most Tyrilleans her frame was slight.

"Mr. Hansing I am Sheena, and I am Virgil's assistant during your visit. Your guide is waiting for you in the main lobby and will escort you to your hotel. Have a pleasant visit."

Hansing thanked her and proceeded to the elevator which took him to the first floor lobby. There he was met by a Tyrillean man in a loosely-fitted tan suit. He was human.

"Mr. Hansing I am Filman, your interpreter, guide and escort," he announced shaking Hansing's hand vigorously.

He reached out offering to take Hansing's case. Hansing raised his hand and slightly bowed, politely refusing his assistance.

Ty Per was probably one of the best kept secrets in the universe. The beauty of this small planet was nearly inconceivable to Earth residents. Although the atmosphere consisted of oxygen, carbon dioxide and other elements similar to Earth, there was an elemental difference that made the sky a bright yellow. Since Ty Per was the second of five planets in its solar system and because all of the planets were positioned closely together, you could always see at least three of the other planets on the horizon. The spectacular beaches with fine red sand and golden waters made it a favorite "secret destination get away." Rachel Jarvis was born and raised in a place famous in all of Tyrill for its seascapes. En Tora was a sleepy village on the main island, Ko Elen, which was the largest in the chain of several hundred islands in the southeastern hemisphere of Ty Per. Ty Per had nothing which could actually be considered a continent, rather it had seemingly endless groups of archipelagos surrounding its globe. As they approached Rachel's village, Filman told Hansing of Rachel's family.

"Rachel is very close to her family like most Tyrilleans. Her village is a very profitable fishing and farming village. Rachel's maiden name is En Sera, which you will find is very common here."

"If the village is so prosperous then why does it look like a slum?" Hansing asked referring to the storm-torn and battered shacks which lined the main dirt street and the malnourished children lurking in the doorways.

"I said the village was profitable Mr. Hansing, not prosperous. The village produces a great deal of revenue; however, the people see very little of it."

"I don't follow you."

"Eight years ago this area was all underdeveloped land. The people were making a meager profit on small farms and were happy. Then a big-minded businessman from Earth came in raving about land revitalization and how this land could be a goldmine with proper development. He told people that he would be more than happy to help them. What he failed to mention was his fee. In the course of revitalizing the land, very expensive equipment had to be brought from Earth and very highly paid engineers had to be contracted to survey the area. The developer would not accept a flat payment for these services; the villagers could have never afforded it anyway. Instead he suggested he take a percentage of the profits. The villagers knowing next to nothing about business accepted the offer. After the deal was made, the developer informed the villagers of costs from the engineers, scientists, and equipment rental agencies to name a few. The bill was several million Earth units. Not surprisingly the villagers could not pay the bills. The developer was more than happy to help them with their problems. Provided of course he was given an additional forty percent of the profits until the debt was settled. Considering the interest on the loan is forty percent and compounded each Earth month, the debt should be repaid in another thirty years. What happened here was very simple: a greedy man eagerly took advantage of hard-working, honest and ignorant people."

"It is sad to think that anyone could be that treacherous to such wonderful people," Hansing said, truly appreciating what these people had gone through.

"The very worst of part of it is that it was a member of their own family."

"I don't understand. I thought you said the developer was from Earth," Hansing said somewhat puzzled.

"Oh, he was from Earth as well as a member of the En Serra family. In fact, he is the husband of their favorite daughter, Rachel."

"You mean…?"

"Yes sir, my employer, Mr. Elmont Jarvis."

Hansing was dumbfounded. The silence which resulted from his inability to speak was broken by the buzzing of Filman's vehicle video terminal. An unfamiliar face filled the screen and addressed Filman, in his native dialect, and faded to black.

"We must return to the terminal at once for an urgent message from Mr. London" Filman said.

"Do you know that this is about?"

"It is possible that Virgil has located Mrs. Jarvis."

"Did he say where?"

"Here on Ty Per," he said as he turned the land rover around on the first road in the center of the village. Hansing was not disappointed to be leaving En Tora. Considering the villager's previous experience with Earth people, he didn't expect a lot of cooperation with his investigation.

Hansing and Filman entered the terminal building and went directly to the communications center on the sixth floor. Communication terminals and display screens lined all four walls of the large room, and two more rows filled the center. Each terminal had a Tyrillean cyborg seated at it, deeply engrossed in his or her work. Filman went directly to the first terminal on the left and spoke to the cyborg Sheena in Tyrillean. Sheena then punched a long sequence on a keyboard. Moments later the face of Virgil appeared on the display screen.

"Mr. Hansing, I have news of Mrs. Jarvis," he said in an emotionless tone.

"Where is she Virgil?" Hansing asked.

"On Ty Per, the island of Ko Elen, in the village of En Tora."

"But we were just there," Hansing said exasperated. "If you knew about this earlier why did you call us back here? We probably could have found her by now," he said somewhat irritated by the incompetence.

"You would not have found her, Mr. Hansing. She is not there in this present time." Virgil explained.

"You're losing me. You just said she was there. What do you mean she is not there in 'this present time'?"

"Correct sir. She is not in *this* present time, but in time eight years ago."

"You're telling me she is in En Tora, eight years ago, *right now*?!" Hansing said in disbelief.

"Yes sir, that is correct. Seventy-three Earth minutes ago my tracking system locked onto a DNA trace that belongs to Mrs. Jarvis. The point of origin was on Earth eight years ago and the destination was En Tora at precisely the time that it departed Earth," he explained.

"How am I going to be able to find her now then?" Hansing reluctantly asked.

"The only way to reach Mrs. Jarvis is to travel to Ty Per eight years ago. Mr. London has already contacted the proper authorities for a permit to travel legally in the past. He is expecting permission within the hour. It is imperative that action is immediately executed before any events occur that can significantly alter the present." Virgil concluded.

Hansing was speechless. He searched Filman's sympathetic eyes for support but found nothing that could prevent that jelly-like feeling in the pit of his stomach. He asked Virgil if Filman could accompany him since he was clueless concerning his destination, particularly in the specified time. He assured Hansing that Mr. London and Mr. Jarvis had already ensured Filman was part of the plan. At least he wouldn't have to go alone. He didn't know Filman all that well, but at least he would be travelling with another human. Besides, Filman's ability as an interpreter and guide would be more valuable than ever.

They departed the communications center and proceeded to the 10th floor lounge to await final word on travel permits. Travelling into the past has been tightly restricted since the inception of time travel. As with Hansing's travel from Earth, it was almost exclusively allowed for travel-related activity. Jarvis must have been really well-connected to get permissions at all, let alone in the tight time requirements. Hansing and Filman made nervous small-talk about what types of intergalactic terrorist must have taken Rachel and how dearly they would pay for their transgressions in light of the men being forced to time-travel to resolve the situation. Filman felt certain that being on Ty Per would be a definite advantage to them because of his knowledge of the environment and the help they could count on from locals. For the first time since he departed Earth, Hansing thought about Ophelia and how he may never get the chance to see her again. Just then, his thoughts were broken by the intercom speaker's announcement for them to report to the closed-loop time compensator. Hansing could see in Filman's eyes that time-traveling wasn't his idea of a really good time either. They did not speak during the elevator ride; nothing needed to be said. They were both terrified of being lost in time for eternity, and any bad guys they encountered when they finally got to in eight-years-past Ty Per were going to pay dearly for making them take this gruesome journey.

They arrived at the closed-loop time compensator and proceeded to the chambers as directed by Sheena. Before they entered their respective chambers, Filman gave Hansing the split fingered peace sign, which was a very old Earth custom popular for hundreds of years. The simple and often overused gesture gave Hansing a strange comfort as he lay once more in the chamber, briefcase clasped to his chest, palms like damp sponges.

The all-too-familiar taste of walnuts filled Hansing's mouth as he awoke in the new chamber. His surroundings looked identical to the ones he departed. The difference this time was the voice on the intercom speaker. It was male and not nearly as refined as he had gotten used to hearing from the cyborgs in his time. He could positively identify the voice as not being human.

"Please depart the chamber area at once and proceed to the reception area," the mechanical voice instructed him. The voice was that of a robot. As he exited the chamber he saw Filman already out of his pod, shaking the cobwebs from his head. Time travel affected people in different ways. With Hansing it was always the jellied intestines and sweaty palms before the trip and the walnut taste afterwards. Filman had to apparently deal with faint dizziness.

A long row of Tyrillean robots and cyborgs were seated at consoles to their left; they were all male and not so nearly detailed as the ones they left behind in the future. As they walked closer to the console, they noticed that not all the people at the terminals were synthetic. A human Tyrillean man got up from one of the display screens and approached them. He seemed to be late middle-aged; his reddish-black hair showed random white streaks and the corners of his eyes sagged from the heavy weight of a responsible gaze.

"Mr. Hansing, Mr. En Sera, I am Jolen For Erin. Virgil sent word of your quest and I am here to assist you. I have ground transportation prepared to take you to En Tora where you will find who you seek." He directed them to proceed to the main lobby area where a driver would be waiting. As Hansing shadowed Filman to the elevator, he realized how much trust he had come to place in a man he barely knew. Then again, he really had no choice.

The drive to En Tora was a bit longer than the one they had taken hours before in the future. Transportation had improved quite a bit in the ensuing eight years. As they approached the village they noticed vast open fields, most of which contained nothing but dirt, which seemed strange because the weather indicated they should have been full of crops.

"Filman, what's wrong here? Why are all of the fields empty?" Hansing asked.

"The farmers have not taken care of the land. This is how it was before Elmont Jarvis came to En Tora. This is why the people were so easily persuaded to listen to his ideas and so quick to trust him. Over the years these people had exhausted the soil to the point that it could no longer be used. They knew nothing about rotating crops, layered irrigation, sectorization or any of the modern techniques and strategies of farming. That all came about in the great land revitalization movement that Mr. Jarvis started. His ideas and technology worked exactly as he predicted. He saved the land. The only problem is that he was greedy and selfish. Otherwise it was perfect."

"Why didn't the government intervene when they realized Jarvis was taking advantage of the farmers?" Hansing asked.

"Because here in Tyrill, when someone gives their word or makes a deal they are bound by honor to hold up their end. Men cannot hide behind governments as an excuse to break their word once given. The people gave Jarvis their word, to meet his conditions to have his technology." Before they got too deep into the village, the men had the driver stop the vehicle so they could survey the area on foot. If there was foul play involved in Rachel Jarvis' disappearance, they wanted to be prepared. As they walked cautiously down the dirt roads, they noticed the village appeared deserted. Suddenly they heard the rallying cheers of people, coming from the other side of the village that was nestled against the sea. They ran back to the vehicle, jumped in, and sped in the direction of the noise.

Thousands of people were gathered in a vast barren field. At the far end was a makeshift stage made from a flatbed truck where one man stood on top delivering a very emotional speech, which the crowd accented with cheers. No one noticed the two men's appearance.

"We'll never find her in this crowd," Hansing said as they slowly approached the stage. Filman did not reply but stopped midstride, his eyes locked on the stage, mouth agape in surprise. He slowly pointed to the man delivering the speech. As they walked closer to the stage, the man on the flatbed became visibly clear. It was Filman. Eight years younger Filman… As to avoid being seen by the Filman on stage, they skirted the right side of the crowd.

"Vicman, this did not happen eight years ago, not anything like this," Filman said.

"What do you mean?" Hansing asked.

"I mean I was here in this village eight years ago and this did not take place. The past has already been altered and it appears to be quite significant."

"Can you make out what the old "you" is saying up there?" he asked referring to the stage.

"I am speaking about land reform and farming tech-
nologies that I had no knowledge of at that time. I am also
pleading for the government to lend us financial support
for an island-wide land revitalization movement. It appears
I am leading these people," he concluded somewhat baf-
fled. They continued until they reached the back of the
stage. Sitting on the ground looking through a tall stack of
papers was Rachel Jarvis. She was alone.

"Rachel, what...what is going on???" Filman asked ap-
proaching her. She looked at them, startled.

"Filman...what are you doing here?" Her reddish-black
hair was long and flowed down her bare brown shoulders.
Her beauty was flawless. Her shorts and sleeveless white
shirt provided plenty to appreciate.

"Looking for you. You're missing. Are you alright?"
Filman asked.

"Of course I am. How did you get here? Did Elmont send
you? Who is this?" she quizzed them.

"This is Vicman Hansing. He is an investigator from
Earth that Elmont hired to rescue you from your kidnap-
pers. What's going on? How did *you* get here?"

"I guess I *do* have some explaining to do," she said.
"After seeing what Elmont had done here, I knew I had to
do something to correct it," she said as she sat back down.

They followed her lead and sat in a small triangle while she unraveled the mystery.

"When I came here and saw how pitiful the people were, I could see that I was the one who had to fix it. I could see how you all blamed me, in your own ways, for bringing Elmont here and for what followed. I went to Elmont's branch office here on Ko Elen, and gathered all of the surveys, report, and other documents about the land reform movement. Then I went to Jolen For Erin with my plan. I knew I couldn't correct things, but with his help, I could *undo* them. I had to do two things: I had to make Elmont's visit here not happen when it did, and I had to give the people here the means to improve the land on their own. When it was time for me to go back to Earth at the end of my vacation, Jolen let Sheena send me back to Earth, but eight years in the past. I talked to my eight year ago self and made sure of the plan. I convinced Elmont to honeymoon someplace other than here. Then I had Jolen and Virgil bring me back here in the past at the same time as our honeymoon to get the information to the people so they would be able to create their own land reform. I couldn't very well do it myself since I was known to be on Earth with Elmont, so I needed the old you, Filman."

"Do you mean I know about this? All of this?" Filman said visibly bothered.

"Not everything dear brother. You know enough so that you can get the money from the government and sell the people on the land reform, and I gave you all of the documents on the technology. You don't know all about the time travel thingy."

"That's a good idea," he replied.

Rachel stood up and placed all the papers on the back of the stage where Filman the speaker could easily find them. "I'm finished now. I'm ready to go back."

The driver took them all back to the terminal, and Jolen put the three of them in their proper place in time without incident. Upon arrival in current Ty Per time, Filman was gradually having corrected memories. He began to remember the missing part of his life and told Hansing he was something of a national hero with the people of Ko Elen and the land reform that he initiated was known as the En Sera Land Reform Movement. Hansing was glad for Filman; he deserved it. Rachel En Sera Jarvis and Hansing reported directly to Virgil when they came back in time and informed him all was well. They were immediately beamed straight to Earth where they were greeted by Elmont Jarvis and Mr. London. They felt a little sorry for Jarvis. They couldn't tell him the truth so they explained that something must have been altered in the trip because they couldn't remember anything. A glitch. Mr. London said he still hadn't found out what happened to Rachel in the first place. Yes, one hell of a glitch. Nonetheless, Elmont Jarvis was just happy to have his lovely wife safely returned. He paid Hansing his bill in full and even added a two-thousand-unit bonus.

When Hansing returned to his office, he found a new and improved Ophelia waiting for him. It seemed that she had spent some time undergoing an upgrade at the Panterra Cyborgenetic Research Center while he was gone. Her cybernetic limbs and implants made her better than she was before.

"Welcome back Sir. I...*missed you* while you were gone," Ophelia purred, batting her lashes and smiling. He noticed her former rather drab clothes were also upgraded to a modern, fresh, sleeveless green dress with a raised hemline, showing athletic, sculpted bare legs.

"Ophelia! You look...breath-taking!" he gasped. Her skin had a healthy glow, and her burgundy hair was now longer, but was elegantly put up.

"Why thank you Mr.—"

"Vic..." he cut her off.

"Sir? I don't –"

"My name. Call me my name now. Call me Vic. Please..." he smiled widely at her. She reciprocated, smiling coyly.

"Yes, of *course.* Vic. Are you pleased? With my *improvements?* She asked apprehensively.

"I am *very* pleased. Yes. Very, *very* pleased." He rushed to her taking her in his arms and kissing her longingly on the lips. She tasted like spearmint, Hansing's favorite. And she knew how to kiss him back, wrapping her wrists around his neck and bending one fine leg at the knee, raising one heel. Where their bodies met Hansing noticed she was warm to the touch. Her emotional upgrade was state-of-the-art and the bill reflected it, but he knew she was worth every unit. He was completely smitten. Hansing decided to check out Ophelia's full range of upgrades on a little vacation. It was kind of like a honeymoon. They decided on New Miami on the recommendation of Elmont Jarvis. It seems that he and Mrs. Jarvis has honeymooned there themselves.

CHAPTER 6
LIFE TAKEN

No matter how many times you tried to kill yourself, the instance you remember most is the time you succeeded. I'd heard it all before I died: "You'll go straight to hell," "it's the most selfish act, and the act of a coward," "what about those you'll leave behind, what about their pain?" "it'll kill your mother," "your wife and daughter need you." Those little trinkets of wisdom kept me alive through guilt for 18 years after the onset of my illness. Due to my bipolar illness, my life already WAS hell. And was wanting relief from this hell really selfish? I think it was more selfish for my loved ones to want to keep me alive trapped in a constant state of torture. But I wasn't quite ready for what I beheld after pulling that razor knife across my wrist, opening my veins into the naked and cold bathtub.

I nodded in and out for what seemed like hours, but was in reality only minutes, until I passed out from blood loss and fatigue. I was sitting on the bathroom floor mat, grounded next to the tub with my left, cut arm, draining in the tub. It was dark except for the night light in the bathroom. I was completely alone. Our four cats had left me to it. I was worried they may eat me after I was dead. I didn't know if that was an old-wives' tale or for real. My wife, Anya, was at work. My 12-year old daughter, Nikki, was in school. Shit, one of them is going to find me. Dammit! Nikki is going to be home first. I didn't think that through enough. I was already regretting not thinking this whole thing through enough.

My body was growing stiff and getting cold but my mind was still conscious. Was I dead already? Just paralyzed by a pre-death haze? My mind, or whatever level of consciousness I still had, was blinded by a terrifying bright light in the darkened room. As the huge ball of light came into focus I made out an angel, resplendent with enormous wings, long dark hair, and a bright glow coming from her skin and full-body covering, sky-blue garment. She didn't speak and had a very sad expression on her face, and I saw streaks of tears coming from her eyes and running down her cheeks. She reached her left hand out and grabbed my right, but my body did not respond. Instead, something I can only describe as a ghost came out of my body by her hand and pulled me to my feet. My consciousness went with my ghost and left my lifeless body behind. My ghost was wearing my dark blue checkered lounge pants and no shirt, same as my corpse. I had no sensation or feeling in my ghost body physically, but had full possession of the faculties of my mind. The angel's icy blue eyes met mine in an instant. I thought I saw deep pain in those endless, reproaching eyes. In my mind I heard her voice clearly.

"I am Saphirra, I am your angel. You have done a terrible thing!" she said. Her lips didn't move. Her voice was that of a young woman and if she was human would have looked no older than 25. Her features were both delicate and elegant.

"Are you my guardian angel? Have you always been here?" I asked in my mind.

"Yes to both questions. I knew you in your mother's womb," she replied.

"What happens now?" I asked.

"You will see the extent of what you've done. All of it."

"Will I…go to…Hell?"

"I don't judge you. That is done at a later time. I am to take you on a journey to provide you knowledge. You took your own life, a very grave offense, but you also have a serious mental illness. You are not separated from God's love. Ever."

"Where are we going?" I asked.

"First we wait. Our first lesson is here. In a moment."

I heard the bell of the burglar alarm ring twice announcing the opening of the front door downstairs.

"Daddy, I'm home," Nikki's voice floated to the second level of our house. After a silence of a few seconds, she repeated, "Daddy? Dad? I'm home." Not getting a reply she would come upstairs to investigate. I couldn't do anything to stop her from coming here, to this room, to this scene, although I tried to will it with all of my strength.

"Nikki! No! Don't come here! Please, not here," I tried to call out but no words came out of my mouth and only Saphirra heard my pleas. I heard Nikki padding up the carpeted stairs and down the hallway into my and Anya's bedroom and into the master bath.

"Daddy?" she called into the darkened bathroom before entering. Her voice was a little shaky, as she knew something was off.

"Nikki, NO!" I tried to push her back out of the bathroom but my ghost arms went right through her.

"DADDY! NO!" she shrieked as she came upon the scene, turning on the bathroom light and collapsing on my now dead body. "DADDY NO!" she was hysterical and crying and screaming, wrapping her arms around the neck of my body, the tears flowing down her face. "Daddy, what have you done??? Daddy, no, Daddy…"

I couldn't feel anything physically, but the pain in my ghost heart was excruciating. My heart was completely and utterly broken. I tried to put my arms around her to no avail. My arms went right through her. "Oh my dear Nikki, if I could undo this terrible thing I would. Anything to spare you this pain, I would," I said in my mind.

Nikki backed away from my body and left the bathroom for the bedroom. She grabbed her cell phone from her belt on her hip and deftly pressed two buttons on the screen.

"Mommy...Mommy, it's Daddy. He cut himself. I think. I think he's dead...I'm not sure...no I didn't, I didn't call anyone, just you...ok, you call and I'll wait for them downstairs...ok...ok...I will...just come home, please." Nikki said, and continued crying and shaking.

Saphirra looked at me and wiped the tears from her face with her delicate hands.

"We're ready to go," she said. In a moment we were in the local hospital's emergency room waiting area. It was full of worried family and friends and people waiting to be seen.

"Is there someone here for Michael Abbott?" a nurse who had just come into the waiting area asked. That was me. Or I *was* Michael Abbott.

"I'm Mrs. Abbott..." a voice called as two people I knew as my wife and daughter walked toward the nurse, visibly shaken to their cores, both dealing with flowing tears.

"Can you please come with me Mrs. Abbott? Is this young lady with you?" she asked.

"Yes, this is my daughter. *His* daughter..." she added.

The nurse led Nikki and Anya through double swinging doors to an area where beds separated by long white curtains hanging from rings in tracks in the ceiling, lined the walls. There was a large rounded-edged square desk area in the center, staffed by various people in scrubs and white doctor's coats. They walked to a closed, curtained-off bed area, where the nurse pulled back the curtain to reveal my body on a stretcher bed, with a sheet pulled up to my chin.

"Mrs. Abbott, I'm Dr. Kern. Is this your husband Michael Abbott?" A man standing next to my body wearing a white coat over scrubs asked.

"Yes, that's Michael...is he?" Anya replied and asked.

"And you positively identify him as your husband?" the question annoyed, tortured and aggravated both Anya and Nikki.

"Yes! I told you it was Michael!" Anya raised her voice.

"Mrs. Abbott I'm sorry to inform you that your husband has succumbed to his wound. He has passed away," the doctor said solemnly.

Anya, upon hearing the news, fainted and collapsed. Nikki tried to catch her mother but Anya fell too quickly. The doctor and nurse rushed to and attended her. Another woman in scrubs quickly brought a wheelchair and the doctor and nurse put Anya in it and continued to revive her. Anya was coming to. The doctor took her pulse and shined a light in her eyes.

"Please, can I see him?" Anya asked.

"Linda, please take Mrs. Abbott bedside in the chair," the doctor said to the nurse. The nurse obliged and wheeled her to the head of the stretcher.

"Michael, I know you can hear me, wherever you are now," Anya said looking around the stretcher and at the ceiling. Saphirra and I moved closer to the stretcher to hear.

"How could you do this to us Michael? How? I know it hurt. I know it was hard. I know you were sick. But you promised me. Promised us. You'd never leave…" her sobbing was too heavy to allow her to speak. "You're killing me too. We are alone now. How could you leave us? Me, Nikki, your parents? How could you?" Nikki came to her side, also crying and put her arms around her, trying to console her. "Michael how will we live? We have no money. There will be no life insurance because you did this to yourself. We can't live without your money. Michael, can you hear me? What can, what will we do?" and with that she broke down again and could no longer speak.

I wanted to comfort her somehow, but was powerless. Useless. I cried ghost tears. My body convulsed from the sobbing, it was so hard. My heart broke again. What had I done? How could I fix this? Saphira pulled my shoulder, turning me away from Anya and Nikki who were crying inconsolably by my bedside.

"It's time to go..." Saphirra said.

"No more, please...no more..." I pleaded.

"We have another place to be..." she took me by the hand and the hospital faded away. I regained consciousness in a room with an open casket surrounded by flowers. There were people sitting and standing around the room talking in hushed tones. Anya and Nikki were sitting and tending to my father who was on oxygen. The three of them looked like they hadn't slept in days. My father looked 30 years older than he was. Anya and Nikki looked cried out.

I was afraid to look at the face in the casket, but I knew it was me and there was a reason I was here. Then I saw her walking into the room. Also looking much older than her 72 years and wearing a black dress, was my mother. She approached the casket and kissed my cold forehead and placed both hands over my body's cold hands that were clasped, holding my black onyx rosary. She cleared her throat and spoke to my body, lying there, waxen, cold, and dead.

"O son, what have you done?" she was talking calmly and evenly. "We've been afraid for you for almost 20 years, but you couldn't resist, could you? Was it the pain? The nightmares? Did you let it beat you, in the end? I taught you better. You were stronger than that. How could you do this to your old mother, your Mommy," she started to cry now, getting choked in her throat. "My baby boy, this was not meant for you. What about your wife? You were everything to her? And my granddaughter? You know she needs you. Even when you were sick, you were a good father. You were Nikki's world too. And me, and your father, even your father, you broke our hearts too. I hope you are at peace now. I hope your pain is over. I hope God will forgive you. Our pain has just started, this pain you've caused us. We will never get over losing you. A mother is not supposed to outlive her child," my dear mother couldn't take anymore and kissed my cold forehead once more, and went to sit with my father, Anya, and Nikki.

"Saphirra please, I've learned, I've changed…I'll do anything…I'll give anything, please is there anything I can do? Any way I can changed this? Any way this can be undone?" I pled with my angel.

"Come" she said taking my ghost hand and the scene dimmed to black.

The next sight I saw was the bathroom where I took my own life. The room dark, except for the night light. My body…no, wait…me; it was me sitting on the floor with the razor in my right hand looking at my left wrist. It had not been cut yet. I had not yet harmed myself. I was warm and alive. I looked at my angel and for the first time saw hope in her eyes.

"Can I go back? Can I change this horrible deed?" I asked.

"You have been given a second chance. Do not squander it. Because now you know the repercussions of your actions. You know how your actions affect others. You have seen the pain you can cause," she said taking me by my ghost hand and touching it to my physical body's hand. My ghost body merged back with my physical being. My consciousness was now one with myself and there was only one me. I looked at Saphirra.

"I will always be here for you Michael, never doubt that. Remember always that I love you and God loves you. You are precious to him and he never wants to lose you. You will no longer see me on this plane, but I will always be here. Peace be with you," and she vanished.

I shook my head, wondering if all that I had seen was real or a dream, and decided that it really didn't matter which, as it served its purpose. I was alive and grateful to be. I looked at my left wrist and at the semicolon tattoo I had recently had put there to remind me that my sentence was not finished; this was only a pause.

CHAPTER 7
KING'S HARVEST

S hip's Log: June 18, 1962

Finally reached land. It is a small island that did not appear on my charts. The landscape is tropical, which is to be expected for the region. Though I had become somewhat disoriented during the storm, I believe I am some 20 degrees north of the Tropic of Capricorn, between New Caledonia and Fiji. My craft, I fear, has little hope for repair. A reef has had its way with *Miss Elizabeth* and has left her with a large hole in her starboard bow and a badly cracked transom. She lies about 40 yards off the western shore, half submerged on the reef. Managed to keep some supplies, some dry clothes, my charts, my trusty knife, some of my instruments, and this log. Taken up shelter for the night in a small jungle clearing just off the beach. No signs of human life at this point. (Elliot Fleishman)

Ship's Log: June 19, 1962

Still no signs of people. Now know what Abel Tasman must have felt like when he explored this region for the Dutch flag. Walked the entire western and southwestern shore today. Nothing remarkable. Found fresh water in several small pools about 200 yards inland from the wreckage. Mangoes, bananas and the like are plentiful. (E.F.)

Ship's Log: June 20, 1962

Explored further inland. Some high mountains in the terrain. Searching for likely volcano. Feeling as well as can be expected. Fashioned a spear from bamboo and tried my luck. None yet. Plan to continue salvage of *Miss Elizabeth* tomorrow, to see if she can still serve some use. (E.F.)

Ship's Log: June 21, 1962

Salvage of *Miss Elizabeth* complete. Tattered sail, rigging, wet bedding, few personal effects. Soon she'll be completely under, maybe another day. Saving some wood for signal fire, in case of contact with boat or plane. Fruits are good but starting to get tiresome. Notice loneliness more on land that at sea. Will travel further inland tomorrow. (E.F.)

Ship's Log: June 22, 1962

Explored deep inland today. Jungle gets extremely thick towards the center of the island. Found a stream and followed it to its source. Incredible waterfall! Also found what appears to be a track plan of some sort. Doubt that it was made by animals. May be first sign of human life. Will explore path and waterfall more tomorrow. (E.F.)

Ship's Log: June 23, 1962

Took provisions and relocated campsite. Now closer to waterfall. Found a series of caves behind and about the falls. The strata appear to be fairly recent, maybe from Eocene Epoch. Seems I may finally get to do some work, though most of my instruments perished in the wreck. Am still taking small samples with my knife. Got distracted from the path. Will follow tomorrow for sure. (E.F.)

Ship's Log: June 25, 1962

Followed path. Captured by natives. Grabbed from behind. Not sure exactly what happened. Not hurt. In small hut. Belongings returned to me just now. Glad log is intact. (E.F.)

Ship's Log: June 26, 1962

Natives seem to be very friendly. Was apparently treated a bit roughly at first because of the surprise at finding me. They weren't sure what to make of me. So far have seen only women. Seem to be from a warrior class of some sort, yet many characteristics of hunters and gatherers. Not completely of Austroloid origin. More similar to Polynesian, yet some European traits as well as Ainu or Mongolian.

Language is a pidgin, surprisingly built around Dutch and the Queen's English. My language background serving me well. Communication really not a problem. Maybe even miraculous is that they have a rudimentary written language. Fascinating! Am being treated rather well. No desire to leave for now and not sure I would be allowed if I tried. Extremely interesting culture. (E.F.)

Ship's Log: June 27, 1962

Remarkable! Whole tribe, consisting of about 40, is completely female. No men anywhere. Also there is no one younger than late teens. They have a queen: a rather tall, dark and lean woman named Alissa. Very exotic and beautiful. She seems as interested in me as I am in her. She appears to be about 30. They tell me all of the men perished during the war, trying to stave off the Japanese. Then where did the 18 year olds come from, I wonder? I'll ask when I know them better. They tell me they are the only inhabitants of the island. Dress is typical of the region, though they all stay completely clothed. Seem to have western influence in modesty. Have been fed well as the women are accomplished hunters. Look forward to learning more. (E.F.)

Ship's Log: June 28, 1962

Queen Alissa. Maybe the most interesting woman I've ever met. I also think she has taken a liking to me. She told me of their deity, a goddess named Livari. She seems to have a lot in common with the Hindu goddess Kali, as she controls nature, be it for better or worse. Alissa told me the lore of her people. Confirms my previous beliefs. Many sailors from the west had been coming for many, many years. Many interbred with the women and several women were taken into slavery. This explains their characteristics as warriors. They fought back. The Japanese came here during the war. They raped all of the women, regardless of age. Alissa herself was the product of one of these rapes. These people apparently seek no vengeance and possess no hatred towards anyone. Their only desire is to be left alone. They don't consider me a threat, luckily for me. (E.F.)

Ship's Log: July 2, 1962

So many things have happened, haven't had time to record daily entries in log. Queen Alissa asked me to be her king! Have accepted without hesitation. Do I have a choice, really, anyway? One of my duties will be extremely interesting. Seems that to ensure continuity of the race, it will be my duty, as their king, to impregnate every woman in the village capable of conceiving and bearing children. Alissa has assured me that she doesn't mind sharing me, as it is essential unless the tribe perishes. Ever aware of the responsibilities of being a monarch, I will perform the duties required of me. (E.F.)

Ship's Log: July 6, 1962

Simple wedding ceremony with elaborate festival afterward. It lasted for three entire days. Initiating the population growth was part of the festivities, for those who were at the time of the month to conceive, including my queen. Am exhausted. Not easy being king. But one must fulfill one's duties. (King Elliot)

Ship's Log: November 8, 1962

Impregnation duties were continuous until now. Twenty-six are in various stages of pregnancy, ranging in ages from 18 to 35 years old. The task was not too unpleasant, and seemed fitting for a king who has settled into marital bliss with his queen. Alissa is also expecting. Life couldn't be better. Days are spent lazily learning the culture and attitudes of my subjects. Have gained a few pounds, though Alissa doesn't seem to mind at all. Do not miss work or New Zealand in the slightest. (King Elliot)

Ship's Log: July 4, 1963

All women have given birth. Thirty-one children in all, as some had twins while others didn't carry to term. Alissa has given me a beautiful baby girl. Named her Elizabeth, after my mother. Total count was 21 girls and 10 boys. Everyone is happy! Celebration is to start on next full moon, which is August 3rd. Alissa said she will make it an annual celebration and call it "King's Harvest" in my honor. Couldn't be happier! (King Elliot)

Ship's Log: August 12, 1963

Celebration was a big success. Lasted the entire week. Finished with a trip to the altar of eternal goddess Livari. All of the man children were sacrificed at the altar, according to tradition, and the woman children were anointed with their blood. King Elliot was offered and eaten by the mothers of the woman children, also according to tradition. Will not need another king for perhaps twenty more years. Elders say this has been the most successful King's Harvest ever. (Queen Alissa) as *translated from tribal pidgin*

CHAPTER 8

GREAT ADVENTURE

It was a long time ago. 1979. Thirty-seven years and one month ago. I have never written down a word of this night, this night in New Jersey in 1979, and have only spoken to a few people about it in all of these years. The details are sketchy I must admit, but the emotion and feeling are tattooed all over me.

My reason for being in Sewell, New Jersey, was to visit with my cousins Debbie and Mary, who after graduating from high school decided to stay behind after my Uncle Jim moved the rest of the family to Fort Worth, Texas. I had taken my SATs about a week after finishing 11th grade, in Maryland, and drove to Jersey directly after. I loved my cousins and their other three younger sisters a great deal, but didn't get to see them enough due to the many moves required by my Uncle Jim's Navy career. So I was really looking forward to the time we would spend together.

The first night, the girls, their boyfriends and I went to see a Rod Stewart concert at the Philadelphia Spectrum. The show was spectacular, with Rod blazing through his rich catalogue, charming the audience with his cool 70's rap, and even kicking soccer balls up into the upper cheap seats. I was thoroughly impressed, just a thrilling night with warm people and a fiery show. But this story isn't about this night...but the next.

Her name was Barrie Ann. Barrie to me. Same age. I had met her two years before at my Cousin Mary's graduation, as she was and is a friend of the family. I had never heard of a girl named Barrie before, and I never met a girl like Barrie after. Captivating. Now, I may get some things wrong here and there, but there is only one person who can refute or confirm my assertions, if she desires. These events occurred 37 years ago, and a fact I am MOST proud of, I was a 16-year-old virgin and I knew less than zero of the romantic arts. Also, my frame of reference is in retrospect.

Debbie and Mary asked how I felt about going to Great Adventure amusement park and let me know Barrie would be going with us. Did I remember Barrie? Huh-what??? DID I remember Barrie??? Does Jack remember Coke??? Hells Bells, yes, I remembered Barrie! But of course the trying-to-be-cool 16-year-old in me just said, "Yeah, I remember her. She's a-l-l-l-right." Inside my stomach was the storm from 'The Rime of the Ancient Mariner" after Mariner killed the albatross. Gracious! I recall a trip to the bathroom for some industrial strength purging. Two hours later we left to pick up Barrie.

La chica esta muy bonita! Actually to say she was very pretty is kind of lame. Excuse my use of adjectives here, but she was gorgeous. Fuck anyone else's opinion, Barrie Ann was gorgeous to me. Let me explain! She was shorter than my 5'10" frame, she was exotic with dark tanned skin, almost almond-shaped golden-brown eyes, and her medium-brown hair was in a Dorothy Hamill wedge haircut. But her body...*shivers.* She had developed quite a bit in this area, with a full, perfect heart-shaped ass, and also full, very full, gravity-defying tits. Excuse my vulgarities, but I'm trying to remain in the spirit of age 16 here. I was hypnotized inside, but think I was maintaining on the outside. I don't remember a single word we exchanged the whole night. But I remember the looks, the feel, the smells, the heat, and the constant tingling in my ball sack.

My total-recall detail of the Great Adventure Amusement Park was a feeling we had a blast, it was dark as hell, and we danced, writhed, bounced and jiggled to the new Donna Summer album which contained "Hot Stuff" and "Bad Girls." It was a sweltering summer night. We were all drenched with sweat. I danced with Barrie every song. Intimately. Far too soon the Great Adventure was over. The Great Adventure in the park that is. We shut it down and were some of the last to leave to end the night. Another great adventure was about to begin.

Now, in 2016, I just Maquest-ed Jackson, NJ, the home of Great Adventure, and Sewell, NJ, the homes of Barrie and my Cousins. It said between 1:07 minutes and 1:17 minutes. Thirty-seven years ago we probably had more like an hour and a half. Trust me, this is the part of the story that defines the reason I wrote it. You will see the need I had to tell this story, even though, like I said, the details are dim and facts may be more fictional. But the feel is real!!!

The minute we got into the back seat of the car, Barrie and I threw our sweating bodies against each other and started kissing. Suction affected our mouths as they slipped around, searching and finding lips, tongues, necks, ears, cheeks...did I mention I was a virgin? I found out recently, Barrie was as well.

Have you ever seen two garter snakes mate? The word is writhing. A constant wiggling to maintain position. Our matching, tight 70's-issue, white painter's pants were moist, damp in the crotches. We were lying in the missionary position, hands literally everywhere, kissing, with my genitalia only separated from her genitalia by two, thin layers of pants, my tighty-whities and her panties, which I decided must have been stupendous. My drawers were soaked from sweat and natural, pre-sex lubrication fluids. From somewhere between her legs came the incredible heat of a furnace. It was like having your hand on the top of a car that had been running for two hours, in the middle of summer. And with her legs open to accommodate me dry-humping her, I felt the full heat from her vaginal land of glory blasting on my junk. I was absolutely confused by the things that were happening in and with my body. My head was swimming. I hope I told her I loved her, because at that time I did.

There were two reasons we still had our clothes on at this juncture. Debbie and Mary. I wasn't going to disrespect them or Barrie by having full-on real-deal sex in the back of a car with Debbie and Mary two feet away from us. And I wouldn't put Barrie in that situation ever. I did hope we would have the chance to consummate this tryst upon our return to Sewell.

My great anticipation was shot to hell when my cousins' car pulled onto Barrie's street, and up to her house. As a gentleman, I got out of the car to walk her to the door, limping from seven-and-a-half inches of frustrated blue steel in the front of my pants. I wanted so badly for the night to never end and for us to have time alone. I got the feeling she felt the same. But it wasn't meant to be. I remember kissing her on the cheek before she went in. My heart sank and my sexual career would still be stunted for another two years. But Barrie was an angel and a crucial partner in my cultivation as a man. We didn't consummate our passionate great adventure and take each other's virginity, but we may as well have. It was a far greater night of sexual chemistry and attraction than my actual first time. I never saw her again, due to shortsightedness on my part. She was fabulous and I think of her fondly and often...

CHAPTER 9
LONG HARD ROAD OUT OF HELL

It's a long hard road out of hell. I could quit there, having told you the lesson I thought that was important at the start of the adventure, but that wouldn't be the whole story and I will not cheat you from your story, my story...our story.

I turned nine-years old during my first year of organized, little kids' football. The experiences were great, my teammates mostly made up from my school friends, all of us mostly staying below the 65-pound limit, excepting for the coach's son John, who often was sweating, puking, pissing and shitting before the game to shed those precious extra ounces to make weight. He was our running back and one of our best players. We did need him badly. The team did great that first year, going to, but losing in the championship game. Our head coach, Coach Greg, bought each of us first place trophies that year, after we lost the close title game, which describes the kind of guy he was. And he had a pool party for us at his house. I believe that is where "the conversation" took place, the invitation was made.

"The conversation" was between my Dad, Coach Greg, and Coach Dan, who we also called Redtop, due to his red hair. Redtop lived at Coach Greg's house with his family, and wasn't going to be able stay any longer. I wasn't surprised since the house held Coach Greg, his wife, and kids which numbered anywhere from three to five. I can't remember past John and his brother, Greg. But there were already a lot of family members in the house and adding Redtop would be squashing them in there more, like college kids in a VW Beetle in the 70's, trying to break the record. So, in the end, my Dad asked Coach Dan AKA Redtop, if he would like to rent our "little bedroom" which my Mom explained meant he would become our boarder.

I didn't know Redtop super well, but he was a nice man. If I was nine, my Dad was 30 then Redtop must have been upwards of 40. Never married, no kids. But he coached baseball, football and basketball, so in that respect, he had a lot of kids. He worked about 15 minutes away and wore a white shirt and tie every day to do office work. He was quiet, but quick to laugh and smile. He never yelled at us. He never said anything mean to any of us. He was very, what I would come to know, supportive. He was one of our assistant coaches on the team, which means he did what Coach Greg told him, pretty-much. I thought that one good thing was that he could teach me more about football before the next season when I would be moving up to the 80-pounder, 10-year old team.

I don't know how long Redtop was living with us before he started sexually abusing me, but it was fairly soon. I was nine. The first time, I was in my bedroom, next to his, when he called me soon after he got off of work. He had already removed his dark slacks, white shirt, red and gray stripped tie and black shoes. He was now wearing a short-sleeved white tee-shirt and white briefs. He was freckled from the top of his red head to his feet. I stood there, clueless as to why he called me, and any sexual reason was far removed from my mind. At nine, I wasn't exactly thinking of such things.

"Buddy, can I make you feel good?" he asked, in now what I know was a lecherous tone.

"Uh, no, I feel pretty good now. I'm gonna go back to my room," I said.

"Wait...Buddy. Why don't you try? For me?" He must have licked his wolf's fangs, as he sat on the bed, sliding closer to where I was standing. I swallowed my Adam's apple harder than ever before. He touched my thigh with his right hand and my...blood...froze.

I didn't speak for the next few hours, but especially the twenty minutes or so that I was in his room, with my pants and underpants around my ankles, lying supine on his bed, my head on his pillow, arms tight at my sides, my breathing shallow, my eyes locked on the far left corner of the room. I was absolutely paralyzed, with the exception of my traitorous penis which was in his mouth as he laid on top of my legs half-on/half-off the bed. I was dead inside. Truly dead. What did I do? What did I *allow* him to do to me? Will I tell my parents? Will I tell anyone? Will this ever happen again? Is it *my* fault? Did *I* make this happen? I am awful. Then...something happened. I felt like I had to pee. So I did. He was very mad.

"STOP PEEING!" he scolded me. I forced him off of me, got off of the bed and shuffled to the bathroom with my pants still around my ankles, and finished peeing. Afterwards, I flushed the toilet and went back to my room and lied on my bed, with a huge, tight, pain in my chest, the pain of shame and guilt. After Redtop went to the bathroom, which I discovered after later episodes, was to masturbate, he came to my room and said in a nice but also threatening manner, "Don't tell anyone anything. We'll both get into trouble."

And that was the complete and total loss of my innocence.

After that first time of being violated, the deed was repeated about 30 times, at various locations, but always the same roles and actions. I was a zombie. From any time he touched me, my blood froze, my mind travelled to the remotest corner of the room we were in, and my soul departed. I was dead, except for the Benedict Arnold part of my body which always betrayed me.

Regardless of how disgusted and abused and violated I felt after every instance, the fear, shame, and guilt always kept me from reporting the events to my parents or anyone else. This causes me an enormous sense of guilt to this day, because I worry and fret over the possibility that this predator may have abused or hurt another child. I have no way of knowing the truth about that because he has every motivation to say there were no more victims. Not knowing the truth and fate of any other alleged children victims was the impetus of me wanting to fight him, in a fair fight, in a cage, like animals, in an attempt to feel vindicated.

I studied Okinawan Karate while stationed there for seven years during my 20's. As part of my training, I learned to fight fairly, in a sporting contest, and follow the rules. More recently I have been training in Krav Maga, the Israeli "Problem Solving" fighting system. Krav Maga doesn't follow any rules, whatsoever. Their objective is to defend yourself and survive a real fight, and anything goes. Eye gouges, groin kicks, strikes to the throat, leg kicks...anything that works. It was probably the most realistic of the fighting systems, but not well suited for a fair fight.

Having been informed by my policeman buddy, Randy, I knew generally where Redtop lived. We had even spoken about Randy and another local officer, and I paying a visit to Redtop so I could ask him a few questions. Do you remember me? Do you know why I'm here? Do you remember what you did to me? Do you admit to molesting me? Are you sorry? Do you have anything you want to say to me? But I worried he might say something that would anger and set me off. Then the scene would be two police officers pulling a 52-year old, accomplished martial artist, off an 80's-something broken-down old man. No honor. No respect. I would be wrong and probably be headed for jail.

There was an option I had read about in some mixed martial arts, or MMA, magazines, of an illegal drug that was working along the lines of testosterone replacement therapy, or TRT, but to ridiculous degrees. It was said to be taking 40 and 50 years off of your age and limitations. Of course you could only get it in South America, and must use it under a doctor's care. If I could take 25 years off, I'd be in my prime. But it is what Redtop could take off that would be incredible. If he could take off 60 years, he'd be close to 20 and formidable. How to get there? My friend Randy had a friend who was a lawyer and a doctor.

"Hi, I'm Rain," I introduced myself.

"I'm Larry," as we shook hands. Larry looked 30 but Randy said he was more like 70. He had a strong grip and a steely gaze.

"Please sit," he said, gesturing to his couch, in his plush office, decorated with light cream walls and dark cherry wooden office furniture. We sat on cherry leather matching couch and chairs, Larry, Randy and myself. Larry wore charcoal slacks and a burgundy polo shirt. It was after-hours, which was appropriate for illegal activity.

"What is on your mind Rain?" Larry inquired.

"I need to make an old man young and a middle-aged man youngish."

"What's the reason?"

"For a fight, an MMA fight, a grudge match." I answered.

Larry paused a moment, looked at Randy apprehensively and then back to me.

"You know these drugs are expensive. And illegal. Here in the states."

"Can you get them. Soon?"

"Yes," Larry said, again looking at Randy. "But it will be $10,000 for the oldest and $7,000 for the younger. Those are discounted prices Rain, for Randy. They also must be administered under supervision. I will provide this service to you as a repayment of a favor to Randy." Seeing my face, he paused.

"Is there a problem?"

"I can only do $10,000. I will take it for the old man and skip my dose. I just don't have it."

"Rain, a 20-year-old will crush you," Randy spoke. "Just worried about your safety."

"Don't worry my friend, my skill is there, and I will take the 30 days just getting into better shape. Larry, can we cover the details?"

"Sure. I will get the youth drug, and contact the other party and propose the contest. You won't have to see him before the contest. I will administer the drug and procure a training facility for him. I will also explain the reason you want to meet him in the octagon and the rules of the fight," Larry explained.

"I remember him telling me he used to box in the Army in Korea, he must have been around 20 years old. This has to be an MMA fight. I'm not a wrestler and probably won't take him down. I'm a striker like him, but I have to be able to use my feet, knees and elbows too, and chokes if I get the chance," I added with a noticeable sense of desperation.

"Rain, 52 year olds don't fight 20 year olds that they are giving away...how many pounds to?"

"Probably 60 pounds. This fight has to be a secret. Secret location, time, date. I want a few people close to me there, you, Randy, him, whoever he wants within reason. Oh and a fight doc."

Randy and I rode to Larry's office together and also rode from his office to my home, since Randy drove.

"Brother, where are you gonna get $10,000 from?" Randy asked.

"I've got it already. From my savings plan at work. I borrowed against myself. The interest goes back into my pocket."

Larry took care of everything, just like he said he would. He met with Redtop, who initially didn't want to do it. Then he didn't want to do it for less than $50,000. What finally swayed him was Larry telling him he would be in the shape of a 20-year-old, not only for the fight, but for about 120 days afterward, until he gradually reverted to his former 80-year-old self. Redtop smiled salaciously, leaving Larry to wonder how warped and demented his thoughts were.

Randy asked, "Rain, what can we do with you, to get you ready in 30 days, to fight a 20-year-old amateur boxer?"

"My skills are solid. I just need heavy conditioning, time to recover, and boxers for sparring partners."

"You got it Brother. My oldest son Ruben is a personal trainer, and he trains in MMA. I will "ask" him to be your fitness coach and corner you."

"That's awesome Brother." I said embracing him. Randy has been my friend for 30 years. I had been his SWAT supervisor back in Okinawa, in the Air Force. Now he was taking care of me like...well...like a real brother.

Training camp. Holy. Mother. Of. God. Ruben was a torture master, but while interrogating me never asked me any questions other than, "Are you alright?" and "Do you have to throw up?" The fight duration was scheduled for three, five minute rounds. I was concerned that my conditioning, or lack thereof, wouldn't make all three rounds. With every cramp and loss of my breath...did I mention that I had quadruple bypass surgery a year before? I regularly asked Larry how Redtop was doing with his training, and he regularly told me that if he provided me with that information he would have to share with Redtop that I was out of shape for an infant and he would most likely be murdering me in the cage in under two minutes. I decided I didn't want him extremely overconfident, thus giving him another edge over me.

Fifteen days to fight night. Great news, I'm not puking anymore during training camp. I am just starting to spar with partners who are 50+ pounds heavier and 20+ years younger. I am in trouble. I am in better shape, condition-wise, but the weight discrepancy is causing a big balance issue in power. I feel like they are hitting me with a Buick, and my love taps are just an annoyance to them. Our strategy for me now is to play great defense and look for openings to throw the heaviest shots I can muster. Every strike has to count because I have to swing for the fences with every strike. Absorbing punishment is going to sap my energy fast and trading is out of the question.

Two days left before fight night. We are done with conditioning. I am in much better shape. I got as strong and built as much wind as possible in a month. My sparring got better. I have a good defense, which I hope can get me to the third round. The third round holds my dignity. I no longer believe I can win this fight, but I think I can be tough and keep my dignity. Show him I'm not scared of him. We are spending these two days with light workouts and strategizing. I am as ready as I am going to be.

⊱✦⊰

Fight day. I had a horrible nightmare about being molested by Redtop last night. It was exactly the same as I described to you already, and I'll spare us both the retelling of the violation of a nine-year old child. If you want to reread it to get your jollies, feel free to go back a few pages you pervert! Anyway, the nightmare was strong enough to stir up the hatred, shame, fear, and anger. I could win this fight, couldn't I? There must be some way. Meh, I hoped it would come to me.

Fight night. Because the fight was a secret and we could only invite a few people, we did it at a local school, an eight–sided black metal cage would be in the center of the gym.

"Are you okay?" Ruben asked, while wrapping my hands in the dressing room.

"Are you gonna puke?" He added.

"Are to ready to kick some child-molester ass?"

"Yes. No. Yes," I replied, repressing a laugh, trying to put my war face on. I still wasn't sure I could win this thing, but something inside me said there was a way. Damn, I didn't know what that meant, but there wasn't much time left before show time.

Randy and Larry came to my dressing room, where Ruben and I finished up and put my gloves on.

"Ten minutes Champ," Larry said to me with a chuckle.

"Champ? You mean Chump? Or Chimp?" I said, also with a chuckle.

"Beat the brakes off of that lecherous motherfucker, Rain," Randy added.

And in ten minutes, a huge bald man, dressed in all black filled my door. "Showtime, fighter," he said then walked away. Cool...but peculiar. No one ever came to check my hand wraps before I put my gloves on. We walked to the cage. Me, walking alone, five paces or so in front of Randy and Ruben. No fanfare, no crowd, no robe, no Walkout shirts, just me in my workout pants, Randy carrying my gym bag with all of my street clothes, and it seemed that we would be sharing a cut man and Larry would remain to appear neutral, for fairness.

After a seemingly long walk to the cage, we were met by the huge bald man, who made sure I had a cup and a mouth guard. He...holy shit! Lost inside my own head, I had forgotten I had an opponent! Walking the same path I just walked, there he was, a young man, early 20's, pale, tall, maybe just over 6'2, muscles everywhere, and...the red hair. Redtop. Fuck, he was big! And looking as happy-go-lucky as ever. I felt small and momentarily all hope drained away. Then I remembered why I was here. Why I went through the last

30 days of pain. I hated this motherfucker. I paid $10,000 to juice this prick back 60 years which will most likely enable him to crush me. I decided to ignore him, and not look in his direction until he was standing in front of me.

I entered the black cage and walked around the outer edge of the floor, all of the way around the cage, stopped in front of where I saw Rueben and Randy, on the inside of the cage. Besides a mild chatter of the group gathered, it was relatively quiet in the gym. Redtop walked into the cage. I turned my back to him and toward Ruben.

"You're ready for this Rain," Ruben said. "You are the only one in this cage that IS a mixed martial artist. The rules favor you." The rules...the rules...the...yeah. The rules don't make up for 30 years of youthfulness and 60 pounds of muscle. I fought and defeated bigger and stronger guys, but that was 25 years ago!

Big, black (clothes) and bald (forever known as 3B) turned out to be the referee too. He summoned us to the center of the cage. There I was, standing two feet away from my perpetrator. Although he was only about four inches taller than me, he seemed closer to seven feet tall. He had a look on his face that I never noticed when I was a kid. It was the look of stone cold stupid.

"Hello buddy. Long time, no taste," he said. My heart stopped for what seemed like a full minute. Suddenly, I was nine years old again. And very scared. There was no way I could win this fight.

"Cease the taunting Red," 3B growled. "You gentlemen received the rules while in training camp, and there ain't a lot to them. Keep it clean. Touch gloves if you want to." Redtop extended his gloves and winked at me. I did not touch his gloves, lowered my gaze and backpedaled to my "corner."

I went to my where Ruben and Randy stood and said, "Ruben, please loosen my gloves...cut the tape a little. They're too tight. I can't feel my hands. Please..." Ruben took the tape scissors and did as I requested, with he and Randy gathering close around me to shield the action from 3B's eyes. He and Randy left the ring directly. The bell rang and Redtop and I shuffled toward each other.

Me: Left jab to his face. Powerful outside leg kick to his left thigh. Inside leg kick to his inner right thigh. Left jab, right-cross combo to his face.

Him: Smile. No flinch. Smile. Shit!

They were all hard shots, perfect technique, but no reaction.

Me: I leapt at him and hit him square on the nose with a Superman punch, and followed with a hard right elbow to the chin. These strikes had all of my 160 pounds in them. No reaction other than a...smile. Shit just got serious.

Him: Digging right hand body shots to my left side ribs. Overhand left to my right ear that staggered me. A right uppercut to my solar plexus, which dropped me to my knees.

Me: Struggling to breathe.

Him: Didn't follow me to the mat. Maybe a little respect for my ground-fighting skills? Maybe he doesn't have a good ground game? Maybe he just wants to humiliate me, crush me where I stand and beat me to a fine powder.

"Get up and engage, Rain," said 3B. "If you don't get up and engage I will have to stop it."

So this is how it's going down? No. I'm up, having regained my wind. I'm foggy. This is going to have to be now or never. I didn't come here to be beat to death. To be humiliated. I stand up the best I can.

"Are you ok buddy? You know, there were many, but you were always my favorite!" Redtop taunted. Somewhere in my cloudy head, I heard a snap. A ring. A siren. A horn. I started backing up from him. He didn't expect that. I struggled but succeeded in taking my gloves off. He didn't expect that either. I looked to 3B and he was screaming "Time!" and he actually ran in front of me and Redtop to stop the action. I swept his legs out from under him and he rolled out of the way to my right and I advanced on Redtop. He smiled. The same stupid-ass smile he would always be famous for in my memory. Shit now has just got REALLY serious.

Redtop stepped in with a right hook full of bad intentions which would have finished the fight had it connected. But it didn't. Instead, my right kick to his groin took all the steam off of the hook and it glanced off my left shoulder. My kick hunched him over, putting him at the perfect level for my flying right knee into his face, backing him up against the cage. Next was my right, reverse, spinning heel kick to his right temple. He staggered to his left and came to rest again the "corner" of the two fence panels of the cage. What the fuck do I have to do to knock this fucker out??? I walked in front of him, pressed him face down with my hand on the back of his head, blood streaming from his face from the earlier punishment, and as his head was coming up to resist my pushing it down, I dropped down with a vicious elbow to the back of his head. That is an illegal technique in a fight with rules, but the rules came off with my gloves. Still didn't drop him. "Time for the finish," I thought. I got up off my ass and from the front, I wrapped my right arm around his neck, using the inside of my forearm to choke him, arching my back and lifting upward, putting him into a standing guillotine. All of this transpired in seconds. Suddenly 3B had his arms around me and was pulling me backwards. I had too good of a choke on Redtop. 3B's pulling on me only allowed me to sink it in deeper, until I heard a loud "crack!" I felt Redtop go limp, and I unceremoniously dumped his unconscious carcass on the mat. 3B released me and turned his attention to Redtop. The doctor brushed past me as I walked away from the carnage. With the broken neck I just gifted him with, Redtop wouldn't get a lot of enjoyment during the next few months of being young, until the juice wears off. From my stomach to my feet, I was streaked with Redtop's blood. The top half of me was covered with tattoos I had recently had done. They were mostly Christian-themed and I wondered if Jesus approved of what I had just done, taking vengeance into my own hands, or did he mean to handle this sinner himself? Then I thought that Redtop had probably done enough to warrant justice from both of us.

END

COPYRIGHT

This book is a work of fiction, although some events, some characters, for better or for worse, are based in reality. With most, there is seed of reality or truth, from which the author added copious amounts of imagination and interpretation. So in the author's case, there IS a resemblance to actual events and persons, living or dead, and it's not entirely coincidental. But it's all from the author's life and he gives his consent full and freely.

Copyrighted by Copyright.com 2016

<a target="_blank" href="http://www.copyrighted.com/copyrights/view/zz00-vyez-ucd2-mtgb"><img border="0" alt="Copyrighted.com Registered & Protected

ZZ00-VYEZ-UCD2-MTGB" title="Copyrighted.com Registered & Protected

ZZ00-VYEZ-UCD2-MTGB" width="150" height="40" src="http://static.copyrighted.com/images/seal.gif" /></a>

Made in the USA
Columbia, SC
16 February 2023

12481428R00072